'Miss Carne!'

'You'll deal with me, will you, Mr Thorne?' Natasha's hands flew to her hair, to the severe chignon. Unpinning the clips, she tossed them to the floor.

Dominic Thorne was staring at her in some confusion.

'Maybe I'll deal with you! Maybe that's precisely what you need... How's this?' She reached up, caught him by the neck, and kissed him fiercely, angrily, on the mouth.

Sarah Holland was born in Kent and brought up in London. She began writing at eighteen because she loved the warmth and excitement of Mills & Boon. She has travelled the world, living in Hong Kong, the South of France and Holland. She attended a drama school, and was a nightclub singer and a songwriter. She now lives on the Isle of Man. Her hobbies are acting, singing, painting and psychology. She loves buying clothes, noisy dinner parties and being busy.

Recent titles by the same author:

MASTER OF SEDUCTION

AN OBSESSIVE LOVE

BY
SARAH HOLLAND

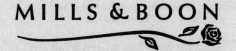

MILLS & BOON

For
Vladimir Ivankiev
My friend in St Petersburg

*MILLS & BOON and the Rose Device
are trademarks of the publisher.
Harlequin Mills & Boon Limited,
Eton House, 18-24 Paradise Road, Richmond, Surrey TW9 1SR
This edition published by arrangement with
Harlequin Enterprises B.V.*

© Sarah Holland 1995

ISBN 0 263 79267 6

*Set in Times Roman 10 on 12 pt.
01-9511-54200 C1*

Made and printed in Great Britain

CHAPTER ONE

GOLD lettering shone on the grey marble walls of Thorne Industries Ltd. Natasha crossed the busy London street, morning sunlight in her eyes, and smiled politely at the young man who held the door open for her.

He gave her a rather unpleasant smile.

She shrugged and walked into the palatial foyer, chandeliers glittering overhead as she crossed to the lifts. As the lift doors slid open, two men in suits walked out, saw her, and laughed secretively, whispering to each other. Natasha ignored them.

It seemed that all the men who worked for Thorne Industries were gradually becoming more and more sexist—or was it more and more blatantly rude? Certainly, their sexual attention to her was becoming annoying.

With her striking Russian colouring of dark red hair, almond-shaped green eyes and high Slavic cheekbones, she had always attracted male attention. The pout of her dark red lips also made men stare, for it showed a deeply passionate nature at odds with her tall, slender body, and the inborn elegance that was almost balletic.

It was a legacy, her mother had always told her, from her great-grandmother, who had been a ballerina in St Petersburg before the revolution.

It was, however, becoming a nuisance, and one which she tried hard to cover up by wearing severe tailored suits, pulling her long red hair back into a stark chignon, and never wearing make-up to work.

Her tactics didn't appear to be working, though, she thought with an irritable sigh, because the men just kept on staring and whispering every time she passed.

Trying to shrug it off, she stepped into the lift.

'Hold it!' A dark, authoritative voice bit out across the foyer.

Natasha looked up, startled, to see Dominic Thorne himself running towards her. Her eyes widened as she stared at this legendary, never-before-seen figure.

He was genuinely gorgeous, and looked just like his newspaper photographs: fierce blue eyes, tough mouth, dramatic bone structure. He could almost have been Russian, she thought, with such stark and powerfully dramatic good looks.

She watched him admiringly, for he was impossibly tall, his hair jet-black, and his powerful body moved like an athlete's, muscles rippling beneath the expensive black suit as a gold watch-chain flashed across his taut, formal waistcoat.

'Thanks.' He strode into the lift as though he owned it—which indeed he did. He owned this whole building, and the business it networked across the globe.

Natasha studied him from beneath her eyelashes. 'The chairman's floor, sir?'

'Yes, please.' He looked at her, a tough smile on his mouth, and the blue eyes roved with dazzling sexual appraisal over her striking beauty and slender, elegant body. 'Do you work here? For me?'

Natasha laughed and pressed the buttons for floor six and then the chairman's floor. 'Yes, I've been here for about six months.'

'On floor six?' His eyes grew intent. 'That's Leachman's department, isn't it?'

'I'm his secretary.'

The steely eyes glittered like blue fire, lit from within as he stared down at her, hard lips parting, and drawled, as though in shocked wonderment, 'My God ... you're Natasha Carne!'

She caught her breath in shock, doing a double-take. How did he know her name?

'Pleasure to meet you at last,' drawled Dominic Thorne with a flash of serious sexual interest in his eyes and deep, sexy voice. 'You wouldn't believe how much I've heard about you!'

The lift doors slid open at floor six, but Natasha couldn't move because she was still rooted to the spot with shock. The chairman? Dominic Thorne himself had heard so much about her that it was a pleasure to meet her at last?

'I'm sure we'll meet again, Miss Carne,' he said softly, 'but in the meantime, I believe this is your floor.'

'Yes.' Her green eyes stared, slanting, almond-shaped and strangely hypnotic. 'Thank you, sir. Enjoy your day.'

She stepped out in her elegant grey pin-striped skirt suit. Dominic Thorne watched her with glittering blue eyes and a mocking smile as the lift doors slid shut.

What on earth had all that been about? she wondered as she walked across the open-plan area towards her office.

As always, all the men watched her as she passed, and it irritated her to be scrutinised constantly by them. One or two of them sniggered as she walked past.

Natasha, as always, ignored them, her face icy.

Reaching her office, she went inside and wondered again what that had been about with Dominic Thorne. Well, try as she might, she would never find out through telepathy.

But she allowed herself an admiring little smile, thinking of his dramatic looks, the stark power of those strong bones beneath tanned skin, and the flash of fire in his steel-blue eyes.

Could almost be Russian himself, she thought again, grinning like an idiot, and then shook herself angrily.

Indulging in romantic daydreams was so dangerous to her that she ought to be shot for allowing herself to do it over a man she didn't know. When would she learn?

Determined not to fantasise about the gorgeous Mr Thorne, she went into work mode, put her handbag beside her desk, switched on the computer, checked the answering service, filled the coffee-machine, and then watered the row of plants on the white windowsill before busying herself opening the morning post.

'Morning, Miss Carne.' Ted Leachman came in just as she finished opening the last letter.

'Morning, sir.' She barely smiled, because she didn't much care for Ted Leachman.

He was a sly, lecherous man of about fifty with a bald head, a paunch, and a taste for smelly cigars. If she hadn't been made redundant from her previous job six months ago, she would leave without a second thought. But as it was, redundancy had shaken her confidence temporarily, and she wasn't prepared to walk out of this job just yet.

'Bring the post in. Let's see what we've got...'

Natasha took the post into his office, aware of his nasty dark eyes roving over her as she sat opposite, taking dictation. They worked well for twenty minutes, but he had to ruin it by being personal.

'I'd love to know what you looked like with your hair down,' said Leachman with an oily smile. 'Especially in a sexy little off-the-shoulder number...'

Natasha's green eyes grew icy. 'Is that sort of remark acceptable in the workplace? I'll have to check with Personnel to see if my rights are being infringed.'

His face went an ugly red. 'I was just trying to be nice. When a man flirts with you, it's not exactly an insult, you know!'

Natasha's full dark red mouth tightened. He'd been like this since she had first arrived. So had all the other men in the office. Asking her out all the time, making passes, innuendoes, sly suggestive remarks.

She wouldn't have minded if they took no for an answer and left her to get on with her life the way she wanted to live it. But they didn't take no for an answer. If anything, no seemed to be the green light for sexual harassment—or something that came perilously close to it.

'The letter, sir,' she said, tapping her pad with her pencil.

'To hell with the letter!'

Natasha arched haughty brows. 'Very professional!'

'A man can't be professional all the time,' he snapped. 'What's wrong with you? I thought you had Russian blood? Aren't you supposed to be passionate under that cold, Slavic exterior?'

'If you don't stop making personal remarks,' she said icily, 'I will have no choice but to pursue this matter through official channels.'

His eyes flared. 'You make me so angry I don't know whether to hit you or kiss you!'

'I know precisely which I'd like to do to you,' she retorted curtly, 'and I will, I assure you, if you don't stop this! A good slap in the face, followed by a lengthy court case over sexual harassment. Unless, of course, you prefer to apologise and return to a more professional footing?'

Suddenly, he blurted out, 'I'm beginning to think they're right about you!'

'Mr Leachman, I really can't——'

'You don't like men, do you?'

Her lashes flickered as the atmosphere tilted abruptly into one that promised something unpleasant.

'That's it, isn't it? You've rejected every man in the building for the simple reason that you're frigid.'

She felt breathless with shock.

'We've all been trying to seduce you like mad, as you know very well, and we thought one of us, just one, might turn out to be your type. But you don't have a type, do you? You're a frigid little iceberg with no time for anything but your pathetic little career, which is cold comfort on those long, lonely nights, isn't it? But what else can you do? You don't like men, don't like sex, don't like——'

Natasha got to her feet. 'Apologise or I'll report you!'

'Go ahead and report me. Every man in the building knows already!' He laughed nastily. 'They call you Natasha Can't!'

She caught her breath and her face drained of colour as everything suddenly fell into place: the sly looks, the sniggering behind hands, the coy whispering and the——

Oh God, the way Dominic Thorne had looked at her with sexual mockery, smiling as he recognised her position, and realised who she was, the famous frigid fool on floor six.

Natasha Can't.

No, no, no, no, no...!

'They've all had bets on you,' sneered Leachman. 'Who'd be the lucky guy to make you thaw out with a quick kiss? I might as well tell them to up the stakes to a million to one, because any man who——'

The telephone jangled.

He picked up the receiver. 'Leachman.'

Natasha stood rooted to the spot with horror, appalled to realise she was shaking, a mixture of rage and humiliation flooding her with such force that she didn't know whether to scream bloody murder or burst into tears.

'Yes, sir,' Leachman was saying into the phone. 'Right away, sir.' He banged the receiver down. 'My God...that was the chairman! Dominic Thorne himself! He wants you to go up to his office, right away.'

It was the last straw for Natasha. Something in her exploded with boiling rage, and she said shakingly through her teeth, 'Does he?'

Turning on her heel, she stormed out of the office, thinking, So Dominic Thorne has decided to get in on the act, too, has he? Asking me up to his office to make a pass at me and see if the rumours are true?

She slammed out of the office, glaring at the men who sniggered as she passed. This is it, she thought furiously. I've had enough. I'm leaving this hell-hole, walking out, job or no job to go to!

But before I do, she thought, jabbing angrily for the call button, I'm going to kick up the biggest scene Dominic Thorne has ever seen.

She knew she was over-reacting, knew her emotions were flying out of her control, but there was nothing she could do about it.

It was all too familiar—the sense of humiliation and helpless rage. To be surrounded by hundreds of people, all of whom had been sniggering at her behind her back, talking about her, placing bets on her, calling her horrible names like Natasha Can't.

It reminded her of Tony.

That was the problem. It reminded her so vividly of what had happened with Tony that she was completely overpowered by the waves of humiliation and rage—she lost all common sense.

She stormed out of the lift into the luxurious corridor of the chairman's floor.

Frigid, am I? Well, I suppose it's better than last time. At least I'm not mad, completely round the bend, a stupid, over-emotional obsessive who everyone knows got fixated on Tony Kerr.

How the memory of Tony suddenly filled her. It ripped aside the icy façade she had built up over the last four years, and made her body shake as the adrenalin pumped violently into her blood and she stormed towards the chairman's office, thinking, I'll teach Dominic Thorne a lesson he'll never forget.

'Good-morning.' The secretary smiled politely as Natasha strode like an avenging angel towards her. 'You must be Miss——'

'Can't!' she bit out thickly. 'Natasha Can't!'

The secretary stared as she strode to the door. 'Miss Can't...?'

'Is he in there?' Natasha asked rawly, not altering her stride.

'Yes he is, but——'

Natasha strode faster and wrenched open the door. 'Don't worry! I'm quite sure he's expecting me!'

Dominic Thorne was seated at an oval desk, leaning back in a black leather winged chair, a panoramic view of London behind his dark head.

'Good-morning, Mr Thorne,' Natasha said through her teeth.

'Miss Carne.' Dominic got to his feet.

'Some mistake, surely?' she flared passionately. 'I thought my name was Miss Can't!'

'Whatever your name is,' he drawled sardonically, blue eyes glittering as he strode round the desk towards her, 'I told you we'd meet again.'

'She just barged in, sir!' The secretary was hovering in a panic.

'Yes, that's quite all right, Miss West. You can go. I'll deal with Miss Carne.'

'Oh, you'll deal with me, will you?' Natasha said in a shaking voice as the door closed and she was alone with him. 'You'll deal with me, will you, Mr Thorne?' Her hands flew to her hair, to the severe chignon. Unpinning the clips, she tossed them on to the floor. 'You'll deal with me, will you?'

'I——' He was staring at her in some confusion.

'Maybe I'll deal with you!' Her dark red hair tumbled free, silky curls falling to her waist as her green eyes spat fire. 'Maybe that's precisely what you need!'

'Miss Carne, I really——'

'How's this?' She unbuttoned her grey jacket, too angry to think about what she was doing, and the powerful dark-haired man in front of her caught his breath as her cream camisole was revealed, full breasts rising and falling below the thin silk and lace.

He stared, a dark flush rising on his cheekbones.

'And this!' She reached up, caught him by the neck, and pulled his dark head down to kiss him fiercely, angrily on the mouth.

Dominic Thorne swayed on his feet.

'See?' She shoved angrily at him, her eyes blazing. 'I do like men! I just prefer to select my own!' Turning on her heel, she stormed over to the door. 'And by the way— you can take your job and stick it up your exhaust pipe, because I won't be staying here another second!'

'Wait!' A strong hand slammed the door shut just as she opened it, and she looked up furiously to see him towering beside her, blue eyes glittering in heavy-lidded, black lash-fringed sockets. 'What the hell am I supposed to make of all that? Why are you giving up your job here? What was all that about?'

'Oh, come on, Mr Thorne! Don't tell me you don't know? You made yourself very plain in the lift this morning. A pity I didn't recognise your smutty tone of voice for——'

'I am never smutty,' he bit out harshly. 'And I genuinely don't know what the hell you're talking about!'

'The rumours that I'm frigid!' she spat, quivering, red hair blazing around her slim shoulders, strands of it soft against the creamy swell of her breasts, the severe grey jacket open still to reveal the hidden sensuality of her silk camisole. 'That I don't like men, don't like sex, and deserve the nickname Natasha Can't! Just because I've turned you and all your despicable locker-room friends down——'

'Now wait just a minute! It's true that I had been told you'd turned down every man in the building. But I did *not* know they were calling you either frigid or Natasha Can't!'

'Liar!'

'Why should I lie?'

'To avoid a nasty court case?' Her voice was fierce with the threat. 'Do you have any idea how completely against the law this behaviour——?'

'If you're threatening a lawsuit, I'd very much like to know what kind. *Are* you frigid?'

Natasha tried to slap his face, her eyes blazing.

He caught her hand easily, strong fingers biting into her wrist, eyes overpowering hers, commanding authority easily over her with his superior male strength.

She wriggled angrily. 'Let me go!'

'A charge of sexual harassment,' he bit out, 'is going to be damaging to both my reputation and that of this company. Now, I want to know exactly what I'll be facing if you do decide to make an official complaint. Is the treatment you've received a genuine case of harassment? And if so, how severe? What precisely has happened? Have the men hounded you for sexual favours? Have they tried to use power over you within the company in exchange for sex? Has anyone assaulted or molested you?'

'Nothing like that!' she said rawly. 'But they have asked me out continually, made insulting remarks when I refused, and now this vile nickname, all the sniggering behind my back, calling me frigid and——'

'Well? Are you frigid?'

'No, I am not!' she shouted hoarsely, mouth shaking, and suddenly the flash of vulnerability in her green eyes made her tear her gaze from his, looking down, suddenly afraid she might burst into uncontrollable tears at any moment.

He stared down at her bent, fiery head for a second in silence.

Natasha struggled not to cry. It was very hard. Waves of emotion, pain and rage and humiliation, were flooding her. Both from the past, and from the present. Suddenly she could see nothing ahead, either, but more pain and rage and humiliation.

Suddenly she couldn't bear her life any more, or what she'd become, because of that swine Tony Kerr.

'Hey...' Dominic Thorne became gentle as he saw her tears and the effort she was making to control them. 'Please don't cry.'

'I'm not going to cry!' Her voice shook with rigid pride.

'OK...' He stared intently at her, compassion darkening his blue eyes. 'But you've been shaken up and you're reacting emotionally. Come on...don't let them get to you.'

Natasha wanted to cry even harder. But she was afraid to accept his tenderness, because it reminded her stingingly of the pity one or two people had shown her four years ago, and it made her feel it was still here, it would never end, she would never, ever be free of it.

'If you're so damned sympathetic,' Natasha asked rawly, stepping away from him, her face hurt and pale, 'and you genuinely don't know anything about this—why did you ask me up here?'

'To offer you a job,' he drawled with a sardonic twist to his hard mouth.

It was such a shock that she just stood there, staring at him.

'I certainly didn't expect this kind of reaction from you, but clearly something else has been going on in this building that I ought to know about.' He watched her with those hypnotic blue eyes and said coolly, 'So why don't you sit down, calm down, and let's discuss the matter properly?' He put strong hands on her shoulders and led her over to the chair opposite his desk.

'I'm not a helpless child!' she said, prickling against any show of kindness or compassion.

'No, you're a tempestuous female,' he drawled sardonically, and then ran one strong hand over her rigid, angry neck-muscles, 'and you're horribly tense.'

'Wouldn't you be?' she spat, hating him.

'Probably,' he drawled, 'but I always have the most satisfying option of punching men in the face when they annoy me. You can hardly do that, can you? So I recommend a good stiff drink to calm you down. What'll you have?' He crossed the room to a drinks cabinet. 'A shot of brandy?'

'I never drink brandy.'

'High time you started, then.' He poured some into a tumbler.

Natasha was still trembling, her slim white hands clutching the open lapels of her grey jacket to hide the silky camisole. She knew she couldn't do the buttons up just yet. She was still shaking too much, so she just sat there, clutching her lapels, and wondering what on earth he had really asked her up here for. Was he serious about offering her a job, or had that been a ruse to stop her filing an official complaint and taking his precious company to court?

'So who, precisely, is behind this sexual harassment?' Dominic strode over to her with a glass of brandy. 'Tell me the names of the——'

'Later,' she said, eyes suspicious in case he was trying to soften her up. 'First tell me about this job you planned to offer me. What exactly does it entail?'

'It's a secretarial position, working privately for a best-selling historical novelist.' He perched on the edge of the desk, watching her with a cool smile. 'My mother, in point of fact.'

Natasha just stared at him in disbelief. 'Your *mother*?'

'I understand you wrote to her a month ago.'

'I wrote to your mother?' she echoed, baffled.

'Yes. Xenia Valevsky. Countess Valevsky. The author.'

She caught her breath, mind reeling as everything slotted into place. Xenia Valevsky was her favourite author, and had been for seven or eight years. She wrote intricately detailed books on imperial Russia, some set in the time of Peter the Great, some Catherine the Great, some leading up to the revolution, but all deeply embedded in Russian life, folklore, language, and richly encrusted with the extravagance of the aristocracy and Imperial families.

Natasha had read every single one of her books, some several times over, and felt deeply connected with her because of it. Eventually, she had written a long fan letter, telling Xenia Valevsky how she admired her, and mentioning that she currently worked for Thorne Industries.

'I have your letter here.' Dominic reached behind him on to the desk, picked up a black file, extracted the piece of paper.

Natasha took it and stared at her own handwriting. 'Xenia Valevsky is your mother...?'

'She has been for some time,' he drawled sardonically, blue eyes glittering, and Natasha felt her pulses race, because he really was wickedly attractive.

'But why the different name? I thought she really was a Russian countess, that her name really was Valevsky.'

'Yes, but it's her maiden name. She married my father, remember, an Englishman called Jack Thorne. As for the title, it's genuine all right, and inherited from her parents. But the land that goes with it is in Russia and now the property of the state, which renders the title almost defunct.'

Natasha nodded, fascinated. 'I'm amazed to discover I've been working for her son all this time without realising it. It's never been mentioned around the office, or in the Press.'

'Well, I'm proud of her, of course, but she prefers to keep her English identity—that of Xenia Thorne, my mother—reasonably quiet. Her public image is so strong. Tragic Russian countess turned best-selling novelist, parents escaped during the revolution, et cetera, et cetera. It's a great image and it sells.' He laughed drily. 'Much more romantic than being born in London, marrying my father, Jack Thorne, an industrial factory owner.' He shrugged broad shoulders. 'And of course, although I've rebuilt the company since my father's death, it nevertheless remains a basically British firm, for all its international tentacles. So she keeps me out of the image-picture, too.'

Natasha stared. 'But—but I would have thought you'd enhance her sales.'

He laughed again. 'How on earth could I do that?'

Unguardedly, she blurted out, 'Because you're so good-looking and so successful!'

His dark lashes flickered, and the blue eyes gleamed as he smiled, a smile so charming that it made her temporarily breathless. 'Why, thank you, Miss Carne.'

A slow burn turned her face a delicious shade of pink. 'At any rate—what exactly will this job with your mother entail?'

'Taking dictation, answering the phone, typing up notes, helping with research.' He gave a wry smile. 'The usual secretarial bit. But there's rather more to it than that, particularly at this point. You see, you will be expected to go to Russia with her.'

Natasha caught her breath with excitement.

'To St Petersburg.'

Her green eyes glittered like emeralds in her white, Slavic face, and she had no idea how beautiful she looked in that moment, how Russian, how feminine, how completely romantic: strange almond eyes shining with excitement, dark red mouth curved radiantly, long red hair spilling around her porcelain skin.

Dominic Thorne stared at her, smiling too, looking suddenly as though what he wanted most in the world was to fall into her eyes.

Natasha blushed again, astonishingly, and said in a strange, husky voice, 'I—I don't know what to say. I've wanted to go to St Petersburg since I was born. It's the most magical-sounding name in the world to me.'

'Then you want the job?'

'Oh, yes, of course! I'd do anything to get it!'

'Good.' He smiled long and slow, his eyes moving over her face, then said, 'Because you seem perfect for it, and I'm certain you'll get on famously with my mother. I had you checked out, you understand. An elementary precaution.'

'You had me checked out...?'

'Yes.' He picked up the black file again, flipped it open, reading aloud. 'Your grandmother was one Anastasia Malakova——'

Natasha gasped.

'Born April 7, 1913 in St Petersburg, the illegitimate daughter of Marie Malakova, a ballerina at the Kirov and your great-grandmother, and her long-term lover, Prince Sergei Kallensikov——'

'How did you get all that information?' Natasha could hardly believe her ears as she heard him reading out the details of her grandmother's birth. 'My God, I haven't told anyone in this office that my grandmother was illegitimate! Let alone the illegitimate daughter of a ballerina and a prince of Russia!'

'I had you traced back to the village in Kent you were born in,' Dominic said coolly, and then nearly jumped out of his skin.

'How dare you?' Natasha shouted, leaping to her feet, eyes blazing like a tempestuous Russian princess's. 'How dare you investigate me like that? Going back to my home town, digging up dirt, making me——'

'Now, just a minute!' he bit out forcefully, standing up and dwarfing her with his extraordinary height. 'I had to have you checked out if I was going to agree to hire you to——'

'You had no right to go to my home town!' Her voice shook with appalled emotion. 'What else did you find out about me? Come on! Tell me! They all talked their heads off, didn't they? Everyone in that stupid little town! They told you all about Tony Kerr, didn't they?' She tried to grab at the black file on the desk. 'Let me see it! Let me see what lies they've——'

'Who the hell is Tony Kerr?' he demanded, slamming a strong hand on the file to stop her picking it up, his eyes blazing furious blue. 'And who the hell do you think you are, talking to me like this?'

Natasha's heart was pounding violently with rage and fear. The thought of him knowing something about Tony Kerr, about the way she'd fallen so obsessively in love with him, humiliated herself in front of the town—well, it was a nightmare even to think about.

'Answer me!' Dominic Thorne bit out harshly. 'Who is Tony Kerr?'

At once, she looked away, breathing hard. 'It doesn't matter.' He clearly didn't know, and if she had any sense she wouldn't push it, or he might just decide to find out.

'It obviously matters a great deal to you.' He watched her with narrowed eyes. 'Who is he? What has he done to make you react like——?'

'Nothing.' Her face was tight with emotion. 'Anyway—I need to know the details of this job with your mother. When would I go to St Petersburg?'

He watched her for a long time, eyes shrewd, and he was clearly aware of her deliberate change of subject, also of the way she was struggling to remain calm in the face of what was clearly extreme provocation.

Suddenly, he seemed to come to a decision to let it slide. 'You'll go to St Petersburg in two weeks,' he said briskly. 'But first, you'll have to meet my mother for a preliminary interview. Shall I arrange it for tomorrow morning, eleven sharp?'

'That's wonderful.'

'Very well. Be at this address——' he handed her a business card '—at eleven tomorrow.'

'Thank you.' She put it in her top jacket pocket. 'I'll be there. But I must stress that I fully intend to resign from my position here as of this moment—whether I get the job with your mother or not.'

He nodded, unsmiling, and his eyes were very dark. 'I accept your resignation. Consider yourself free to go. But before you do, I want the names of everyone involved. Tell me precisely what happened and who was directly responsible.'

Natasha told him, her voice cool, clipped and precise.

'Do you want to make an official complaint?' he asked when she had finished. 'You obviously have a solid case. The only problem is—how many of the other men will come forward to testify on your behalf?'

'None, I should think.'

'Because you hurt their egos,' drawled Dominic Thorne, a gleam in his blue eyes as he looked down at her ravishingly unique and dramatic face. 'A shame they weren't here to witness your very exciting display of red-blooded passion!'

'I was in a temper.' She felt deeply embarrassed. 'I didn't know what I was——'

'Oh, please,' he drawled sardonically, 'don't apologise. It was a scene from one of my favourite office fantasies.'

'Oh...!' Her face burnt crimson and she looked away, unable to maintain eye contact, her fingers fumbling with the still loose lapels of her open jacket, aware of his blue eyes roving insolently down to probe the shadowy hollow between her breasts.

'I only wish I could stay here with you a little longer to discuss it, but I'm afraid I have a board meeting in precisely——' he glanced at the Cartier watch on his hair-roughened wrist '—seven minutes.'

Natasha recognised dismissal when she heard it. 'Yes, of course.' She got to her feet, turning to walk to the door.

He followed her. 'Send Leachman up to me right away.' Another glance at that expensive watch. 'I've just got time to execute him before the board meeting.'

'Execute him?' Natasha turned at the door.

'Of course.' He towered over her, face dramatically good-looking and very exciting. 'You don't seriously think I'm going to allow him to stay here after this, do you? He's out. Consider it done.'

Her eyes seemed to stare adoringly, of their own accord, up into that hard, handsome face.

He smiled down at her. 'And one other thing...' His gaze lowered intimately to her breasts, his voice growing rough with sexual attraction. 'Best do this up before you go back down to the den of wolves...'

Natasha's whole body pulsed with waves of shimmering pleasure as he slowly, surely, began to button her jacket up, flicking his gaze from her eyes to the scented hollow between her breasts, then up to her dark red mouth, then back to her breasts while she stood there, heart pounding, feeling her nipples erect and shivers run up and down her skin.

'See you soon,' he murmured, and bent his dark head to brush a brief, burning kiss on her mouth. 'Just returning the compliment,' he drawled, and slid one strong hand to her naked throat, inciting shivers of pleasure as he bent his head again, and kissed her passionately.

'Oh...!' She succumbed without meaning to, almost as though she were hypnotised, her arms going around his strong neck as he pulled her hard against his powerful body.

The hot onslaught of his mouth made her dizzy, and she clung to him, breathing faster, aware of his heartbeat thundering as his strong hands moved firmly, possessively over her slender body.

Suddenly, the telephone on his desk rang.

'Damn!' he said thickly, wrenching his hot, commanding mouth from hers and glancing over one broad shoulder.

Natasha swayed as he released her, and fumbled with the door-handle, going out, his touch still on her skin, his kiss still lingering on her lips, his presence still making her tremble with excitement, romance, magic...

And he was part-Russian, too, just as she was.

I knew it as soon as I saw him, she thought dazedly. My God, he's everything I've ever wanted in a man, everything I've ever dreamt of, everything I've——

What rubbish! she thought in sudden fear, as she stopped herself weaving fantasies around a man she hardly knew.

I just got carried away because he showed some interest in me, and kissed me. He's a very attractive, desirable man, and of course I got carried away in a stupid romantic daydream.

But it doesn't mean anything. It certainly doesn't mean I'll ever see him again, even if I do go and work for his mother.

Certainly, she wasn't going to let herself get into the same mess she got in over Tony! Oh, dear me, no, she thought furiously as she strode out of the lift and back to her own office.

No more fantasies for me, no more obsessive love without foundation, no more love, full stop.

None.

CHAPTER TWO

THE next morning, she was smartly dressed in a severe black tailored skirt suit, buttoned right up to the neck, with a small, elegant frill at the throat and discreet pearl ear-rings in her ears. As always, she wore her long red hair swept up into a cool chignon.

Xenia Valevsky lived in a beautiful white house in an exclusive London square. A butler answered the door on Natasha's ring, and ushered her into a very formal drawing-room furnished entirely in French antiques.

Natasha had rarely seen such luxury outside a magazine. She came from an ordinary family—albeit with an extraordinary past.

She felt slightly out of place, therefore, sitting on an elegant yellow brocade sofa with little gold claw feet, while the sunlight shone in through the long windows on to fabulous, elegant antiques.

'Ah!' Countess Valevsky entered. 'Miss Carne!'

Natasha looked up to see her heroine in the flesh, and she was awed for a second, staring at her with a radiant smile, for she was everything Natasha had always thought she would be.

Tall, slender, very elegant, the Countess wore a smart white skirt suit, very similar to Natasha's, buttoned up to the neck, two strings of pearls across it, her dark hair swept up in an elegant chignon.

'How wonderful to meet you at last!' The Countess swept over to her as Natasha stood up, and held out her hands. 'I've been dreaming how you would look, and I can hardly believe that you're just as I pictured you.'

'And you're every bit as beautiful as your photographs, Countess.'

'Do, please, call me Xenia.' She moved past her to the blue and yellow brocade armchair. 'I've asked Bowers to bring some tea. Did my son tell you about the research trip to St Petersburg?'

Natasha at once found herself enthusing over the prospect, and before long they were both swapping love-stories over St Petersburg, Imperial history, and Russia.

Bowers brought the tea on a silver trolley.

'Just wait until you see Peterhof!' Xenia was saying as she poured from the silver pot. 'It's the Russian equivalent of Versailles.'

'I've seen photographs of it.'

'And, you know, Peter the Great's study is still there,' Xenia informed her. 'I've seen it. Actually stood in the same room that he did, when he made all those plans. What a marvellous tsar he was.'

They talked on and on, skipping from one topic of conversation to the next. They clearly had similar minds, similar personalities, similar interests.

Time slipped by unnoticed.

Xenia called for more tea.

They talked about the tragedy of the Romanovs, and Natasha was thrilled to discuss in detail the last months of the Tsar, his imprisonment first in Tsarskoe Selo, then in Tobolsk, and finally at the Impatiev house in Ekaterinburg, where the family were slain.

'I can see you're going to be my dream secretary.' Xenia was as excited as Natasha. 'I've always longed for a secretary who understood Russian history as you do.'

'I've spent my whole life reading every book on Russian history I could lay my hands on,' Natasha confessed with a smile.

'Of course you have. With your ancestry.'

'It's mainly because I look so much like the Russian side of the family,' Natasha told her. 'I'm apparently the living image of my great-grandmother.'

'She must have been very beautiful.'

Natasha laughed, thinking herself not very beautiful at all.

'Dominic remarked on it, too,' Xenia continued. 'He said you were the most strikingly beautiful woman he'd ever seen. And very Russian.'

Her heart skipped a stupid beat. 'Well…that was very kind of him.'

'He's always been irresistibly attracted to Russian-looking women. He was even in love with one, once. A ballerina, funnily enough. Kyra, her name was. I thought for some time that he would marry her.'

'Do you think he's the marrying kind?' Natasha asked wryly, somehow doubting that a man like Dominic Thorne would ever settle down.

'He's thirty-seven now, and beginning to think of having a family. But it's difficult for him, because he wants the woman to have Russian blood, or at least some Russian connection. And that's not so easy——'

The doorbell rang softly in the marble hallway.

'Who on earth can that be?' Xenia frowned, looking at her elegant watch, then gasping, 'Oh, no, I completely forgot! Dominic said he'd drop by for lunch!'

Natasha's heart leapt violently, and a second later she heard his deep, dark, gorgeously masculine voice in the hall.

No fast-beating hearts, she thought angrily, struggling to control her responses. No blushing and no pulse-soar, and definitely no smiling at him like a besotted idiot.

Dominic Thorne isn't interested in you, he never will be, and you're not interested in him, either. You mustn't be interested in him or you'll do the same thing, all over again, that you did with Tony. Besotted, obsessed, fixated... and then people find out and you're humiliated.

So ignore his stunning looks, his intellect, his dynamism, his sex appeal, his power and his Russian ancestry. Stop being romantic and start being a bit more level-headed.

'I know!' Xenia said. 'Why don't you stay for lunch, too?'

'Oh, no, I really couldn't.'

'Why not? I'm sure Dominic would be delighted, and so would I.'

'I have an appointment with my bank manager at two o'clock,' Natasha remembered with relief.

'Oh, what a shame that——'

The door opened and Dominic Thorne, a superb masculine presence, strode in, dominating the room at once with his height and power and air of effortless authority.

'Still here?' he drawled, smiling dazzlingly at Natasha, whose heart leapt like mad in response. 'I take it you've got the job, then?'

'Yes, I have.' Natasha got to her feet, her face icily serene, determined not to let him know how devastatingly attractive she found him.

'Good,' he drawled. 'I look forward to running into you frequently from now on.'

'How kind.' Natasha's voice dripped ice.

He frowned, because of course she wasn't even smiling at him, and he had given her the kind of smile that made her do back-somersaults inside.

There was a brief, tense pause.

'Well!' Xenia clapped her elegant hands together. 'Shall we have a little champagne? To seal the bargain and welcome Natasha into the fold?'

'Yes, why not?' Dominic gave a hard smile, still frowning, and turned to walk to the door, opening it, drawling over one broad shoulder, 'I'll tell Bowers to set the table for three, shall I?'

'No, I can't stay for lunch,' Natasha clipped out coolly. 'I have a previous engagement.'

He paused in the doorway, eyes narrowing on her, aware of her sudden icy hostility and not understanding it, particularly after the passionate kiss she had given him yesterday when she left his office.

Then he went out, closing the door with an angry click.

Natasha relaxed, turning to her new employer. 'When do we leave for St Petersburg? Where are we staying?'

'We leave in a fortnight, and we'll be staying at the Hotel Europe, right in the centre of the city.'

Dominic's footsteps came clicking angrily back down the hall.

Natasha's mouth went dry. 'Is it a nice hotel?'

'Ravishing. Malachite pillars, gilded mirrors, hot and cold running waiters . . .'

The door opened and Dominic strode in, hard-faced and holding a bottle of Bollinger, the neck smoking, three champagne flutes in his strong hand.

'But Dominic will give you the details next week, won't you, darling?'

'Yes,' he said tersely, putting the glasses down on the gold oak coffee-table and pouring champagne into each of them.

Xenia frowned at him, then at Natasha.

He handed Natasha her glass, his face tough. 'I'll drop in at your flat some time next week with the details. Meanwhile, I need you to fill out a form for the entry visa.'

'Yes, of course,' she said coldly.

Straightening, he took the form from his inside jacket pocket, giving her a glimpse of that powerful chest, the taut stomach, and the dark grey silk lining of his jacket, the unmistakable black-silver label reading Gieves and Hawkes, No. 1, Savile Row.

Natasha took a pen from her handbag and sat down to fill the form out, marvelling at the excitement she felt on seeing all that Russian writing, so foreign, so romantic, so magical.

When she had finished, she glanced at her watch. 'I'm afraid I really must dash.'

'I'll see you to the door,' Dominic said curtly, and her pulses hammered as she tried to look cool, kissing Xenia goodbye, saying how much she was looking forward to beginning work with her in a fortnight, then, riddled with tension, walking out with Dominic right behind her.

He closed the drawing-room door.

Natasha increased her pace, hurrying to the front door.

'Just a minute!' Dominic bit out under his breath, catching up with her in three long strides, grabbing her arm, spinning her to face his blazing blue eyes. 'What the hell is wrong with you? Why am I suddenly getting the ice-maiden stuff?'

'I don't know what you mean,' she said tightly, stung by his choice of words and the memories of yesterday they brought back.

'Don't lie! Yesterday, you kissed me passionately, poured out your heart to me, then kissed me even more passionately. Today you're ice from the neck down. No, from the eyebrows down—it's even more noticeable looking into those eyes.'

'Then don't look into them, Mr Thorne!'

'Mr Thorne?' He laughed harshly. 'Call me Dominic, or I'll start to think you kiss every man you meet the way you kissed me!'

Her eyes flared angrily. 'You know perfectly well I only did that because I was so upset!'

'The first time—yes.'

Hot colour burnt her face as she remembered the passion with which she had surrendered to his kiss yesterday, the feel of that hard, commanding mouth on hers, the feel of his powerful body.

'So what's going on?' he said thickly, lowering his head closer to hers. 'Why are you suddenly so hostile?'

'I'm not hostile.'

'Natasha, you are not the woman I met yesterday.'

'I could always produce my passport.'

'Don't be funny,' he bit out, staring angrily into her eyes. 'You know damned well what I mean.'

She raised her head, face tight with defensive anger. 'Look—I've just accepted a job with your mother. It would hardly be appropriate for me to go around kissing her son every five minutes!'

'I'll be the judge of that,' he drawled with a sardonic smile. 'I rather enjoyed your kisses yesterday, and I want to enjoy them again.'

Nothing he could have said could have frightened her more. It meant he planned to chase her, to kiss her, to whisper sweet nothings in her ears...

And that would do it, that would make her flip her tiny lid again, that would feed the obsession she already knew could develop for a man as gorgeous and unattainable as Dominic Thorne.

'Well, you can't!' she said icily, and wrenched open the front door, her face a white mask of scorn and contempt. 'Kindly keep your hands off me from now on, Mr Thorne. I am *not* interested!'

Turning, she strode away down the path, her face rigid with determination, but she was both shocked and hurt when he didn't try to follow her, because of course she thought he was wonderful, gorgeous, dazzlingly attractive, and she wanted him.

Her hand shook as she unlocked her little blue sports car, slid behind the wheel of it, and drove away without looking back.

God help me, she thought, her heart still pounding with excitement and fear. I feel more attracted to him than to any man I've ever met—and that includes Tony the Swine Kerr.

Look how she had flipped her lid over Tony, and she had barely found him attractive at all in the beginning. He had just been so attentive, so charming, and so unattainable, that in the end she had fallen hook line and sinker for him.

Unattainable was the key word, of course. She had worshipped him like a teenage fan with her idol, and the fact that he had never made love to her had made her obsession worse.

But Dominic Thorne was even more unattainable...

He was everything she had yearned to meet in a man, and far too eligible to take notice of a boring little secretary like her.

Tall, strong, intelligent, sexy, dynamic, sensitive, charming, gorgeous—and with a romantic Russian background, just like hers. He could have been handmade for her by fate.

Yes, she thought grimly, handmade for me to fall for, because that's what'll happen if I don't fight him. And before I know it, I'll be feeding an obsessive love for him, just like I did for Tony.

Feeding it.

Like a secret plant, kept in the darkness of a hot-house, pouring water on it every hour, talking in hush-hush whispers to it, words of love and desire making it grow and grow until it became a monster...

I must not let myself fall for Dominic Thorne, Natasha told herself fiercely.

I must not let that obsessive streak out, ever again.

I mustn't even kiss him again.

Not ever.

He came to her flat ten days later.

She thought she was ready for him, because he had telephoned earlier to let her know he was on his way, and his terse, cold tone of voice hurt something inside her, even while she reciprocated, equally cold and impersonal.

But nothing she did could prepare her for Dominic, because she already secretly wanted him, already secretly found herself daydreaming about him, about his kiss, his smile, his ready wit, his powerful body, and his strong, handsome, Russian face.

Determined to look attractive herself, she changed quickly into a formal trouser suit in dark green, scraped her long hair back into its cool chignon, and put a little make-up on, her hand unsteady as she applied mascara to her dark red lashes.

Then she went into the living-room, pacing like a restless, fiery gazelle, trembling inside with excitement at the thought of seeing him again.

'What are you up to?' Dolly, her flatmate, asked curiously.

'Mr Thorne is coming round,' Natasha told her non-committally, 'to give me my visa and the details of my flight to St Petersburg.'

'So why get all togged up to see him?' Dolly eyed her formal suit with a frown. 'It's just a brief, casual visit, isn't it?'

'I imagine so.'

Dolly laughed at her formal words. 'You imagine so! Honestly, you are a hoot!'

Dolly Day was exactly like her name: a beautiful blonde bombshell. She was one of those warm, naturally glamorous, naturally exciting women with tremendous personality. She had never been deeply hurt by life, and hopefully never would be.

Natasha frequently envied her as she breezed her way through life, surrounded by friends, swamped by admiring men, throwing parties and getting drunk and laughing at herself when anything went wrong, and never having a cross word for anyone.

She was the perfect friend for Natasha, who had been so bitterly hurt that she often wondered if she would ever recover, and was afraid that the answer was very probably—never.

At least while Dolly Day was with her, Natasha would feel the sunshine.

The doorbell rang.

Natasha jumped, nervous eyes flicking round as she froze in the centre of the living-room.

'Want me to get it?' Dolly asked with a smile.

'No, I...' She ran a slim hand over her smooth chignon. 'I'll go.'

By the time she reached the front door, her palms were sweating. She smoothed them on the legs of her trousers, took a deep breath, told herself she had nothing at all to be afraid of, and opened the front door.

His face was so powerful to her now that her heart beat with sickening speed just at the sight of him, and it was difficult to keep her cool. She wanted to kiss him. Her eyes darted with secret passion to his mouth.

'Hi,' he drawled coldly. 'May I come in?'

'Of course.' She stepped back, cold and expressionless.

Dominic walked inside, irresistibly sexy in black jeans and black V-necked sweater, the sleeves pushed up a touch to show tanned, hair-roughened forearms, the V-neck showing his powerful chest.

Natasha's eyes raced over his body with hot, secret longing. She closed the front door behind him, pushed her hands into the pockets of her elegant trousers, and looked up at him through dark lashes, wondering if she was in as much danger from him as she thought she was.

'Do you have the entry visa for me?'

He towered over her, eyes hard. 'Yes. Are we to discuss everything here in the hallway?'

'No, please follow me.' She led him to the dining-room along the hall, preferring to be alone with him under formal conditions. 'May I offer you some tea or coffee?'

'I'd rather have a shot of whisky,' he drawled, tossing the file in his hand on to the mahogany table.

Natasha's lashes flickered. 'I'll have to ask Dolly.'

'Dolly?' His hard mouth twisted in a sardonic smile.

'My flatmate. If you'd like to wait here, I'll——'

'Can't I meet Dolly?' he drawled, following her out of the room. 'I love dollies!'

Jealousy immediately struck at her vulnerable heart, and as she pushed it away she felt it come thundering back, because she suddenly realised how completely different from her Dolly was, and how much Dominic might prefer her vibrant, open warmth to Natasha's hurt, damaged personality.

'Of course,' she heard her icy voice say, and walked elegantly ahead of him to the living-room, opening the door and saying tightly, 'Dolly, Mr Thorne wanted to know if we had any whisky here?'

'Whisky?' Dolly turned from the bookshelf, blonde hair a lion's mane around her pretty face. She was sexily dressed in black miniskirt and blue silk blouse. Pale pink lipstick shimmered on her luscious, smiling lips. 'I think Bobby left a bottle here the other night.'

'Your boyfriend?' drawled Dominic Thorne, smiling at her with a glitter in his steel-blue eyes.

Natasha watched grimly, jealousy searing her blood.

'Oh, hi!' Dolly gave him a warm smile. 'You must be Mr Thorne. I've heard tons about you. Come on in.'

'Thank you.' Dominic shot Natasha a mocking glance, as though he knew she was raging with silent jealousy, and extended a strong hand to Dolly. 'It's a real pleasure to meet you.'

'And you.' Dolly shook his hand, smiling openly. 'Hey—are you sure you wouldn't rather have a beer?

Bobby left loads round here. He and the boys came round to watch the football.'

Dominic laughed, eyes moving admiringly over her figure. 'You have a lot of boyfriends, then?'

'They're boys and they're friends.' Dolly laughed. 'But that's about it. So what'll it be—whisky or beer?'

'Whisky will be fine.' He thrust his hands into the pockets of his jeans, shot a sidelong glance at Natasha's tight, angry face. 'I've never met two such different women sharing a flat together. Does it work well?'

'Oh, wonderfully well.' Dolly unearthed a bottle of Johnnie Walker Black Label from under a pile of magazines.

'But you're so bright and bubbly,' drawled Dominic, while Natasha stood there, hating him, 'and Natasha is so cool and mysterious.'

'You called me tempestuous the other day,' Natasha snapped, eyes flashing passionate, jealous green. 'Make up your mind!'

He looked at her, a sardonic smile on his mouth. 'Temper, temper...' he said softly, mockingly, and his smile deepened as he watched the hot, betraying colour rush up her face.

'Here we are!' Dolly handed him the bottle of Johnnie Walker and a glass. 'Not much left, I'm afraid.'

'Thanks.' His eyes roved over her with admiration again. 'Where do you work, Dolly, and who——?'

'Dolly is going out shortly,' Natasha cut in tightly, 'and we mustn't keep her. She has to be ready when her boyfriend arrives.'

'She looks stunningly ready to me,' drawled Dominic, eyes roving with even more blatant sexual admiration over her.

'Would you please come back to the dining-room with me, Mr Thorne?' Natasha snapped. 'I believe we have a lot to discuss!'

Turning on her heel, she strode angrily along the hallway, hearing Dominic say an amused goodbye to Dolly before following her, catching up with her easily on those long, muscular legs of his.

As soon as he entered the dining-room, Natasha closed the door behind him and walked elegantly to the table, hating him for flirting with Dolly and tempting her to make such a fool of herself with her pathetic, absurd and completely unjustified jealousy.

'You said my visa had arrived...?' Her voice was icy.

'Yes, it has.' He moved to the table too and sat down opposite her, watching her from underneath those heavy, Slavic eyelids.

Natasha felt suddenly uncomfortable. The gleam in those steel-blue eyes sent her pulses racing and her stomach somersaulting. She needed to know what he was thinking.

Irritably, she said, 'Why are you just staring at me like that?'

'Because I'm intrigued by your behaviour,' he said softly, arching black brows. 'First you kiss me passionately, then you reject me with icy hostility—and then you seethe with jealousy when I flirt with your flatmate.'

Scarlet colour suffused her cheeks. 'I can assure you I did not feel remotely jealous!'

'Hmm.' His smile was sardonic. He toyed briefly with the empty glass in front of him, studied the whisky bottle, but did not pour himself any. Then he looked back at her, and there was a glint of mockery in his blue eyes that made her temper flare.

'I wasn't jealous!'

'Did I contradict you?'

'No.' Her mouth tightened. 'But I noticed a look in your eyes that made me think you——'

'And you notice a lot about me, don't you?'

She fell silent, lashes flickering.

'I mean,' he drawled lazily, 'for a woman who feels nothing for me and doesn't want to get involved.'

At once she looked away, heart thudding fast, realising for the first time just how clever, how shrewd, how very perceptive this man was.

'You're a mass of contradictions, aren't you?' He was watching her with those steel-blue eyes. 'That icy, polished façade hides a very tempestuous woman. So far, I've seen you show blazing fury, intense passion, seething jealousy—and I've even seen you burst into tears. Perhaps it's good that you don't want to get involved with me. If you did, I——'

'But I don't want to get involved with you.' Her strange, intense green eyes flashed up with glittering hostility at him. 'I don't want to get involved with anyone.'

'Apparently not,' he murmured, watching her intently. 'Certainly, no man at the office managed to get anywhere with you. And you don't have a boyfriend, do you? I know, because I had you checked out, remember, and there was no mention of any man in London.'

Natasha looked at the polished surface of the table, rigid with tension, hating him for being so damned clever, afraid of where he was leading with this line of thought.

'You've lived in London for four years, haven't you?'

'Yes,' she said tightly.

'And no man, in all that time?' He clicked his tongue softly, shook his dark head, smiling like a Siberian tiger ready to pounce. 'How do you cope with all that emotional energy? You must be like a pressure-cooker, getting ready to explode.'

She sat there silently hating him and saying nothing.

Dominic watched her, waiting for an answer.

The clock ticked softly on the mahogany mantelpiece.

'But this is so exciting!' Dominic said softly, eyes deadly. 'I do love mysteries, and I feel sure you're one of the biggest mysteries I've ever met. I simply must try to unravel you.'

Natasha shot him a look of ill-concealed hatred.

'It must be something to do with your past,' he murmured, eyes narrowing in thought. 'But it can't be here in London, or my agents would have found it. Therefore, it must be before you came to London. QED.'

'Will you just go away and mind your own business?' she said with sudden fierce dislike, because he was much too clever to be allowed to run amok through her past with those damned agents of his.

'I was right, then,' he said sardonically, smiling. 'And it must be something to do with a man, or you wouldn't now be so determined to avoid them at all costs.'

'Will you just mind your own——?'

'So what exactly happened to make you shy away from men? Obviously, there are a number of things that could have caused it. So let's tick them off. After all, you know what Sherlock Holmes maintained: eliminate the impossible, and whatever you are left with, no matter how improbable, must be the truth. So let's start with the possibility of some kind of sexual attack.'

'Oh, for God's sake!'

'Well, I did consider sexual violence when I first met you, but not for very long because you're the one who kissed me—and very passionately, too.'

Her eyes flared. 'You know why I kissed you!'

'Your motivation is not under the microscope, sweetie. Let's just stick to the point.'

'The point is that I want you to go!'

'And the point is that somebody in the past—some man—inflicted some kind of damage on you which makes you avoid getting involved. It can't have been sexual damage, because sex clearly isn't the barrier.'

'Will you stop this?' she demanded fiercely, as fear rose in her.

'No, it must be emotional, because that's what you're really afraid of, isn't it? You're afraid of getting emotionally involved with a man, any man, doesn't matter——'

'I asked you to stop!'

'And if that's the case, then it must be a man in your home town in Kent who——'

'Stop it!'

'A man in Kent who hurt you so badly that——'

'Shut up!' Natasha shouted hoarsely and got to her feet with such sudden violence that her chair toppled backwards, crashing into a glass cabinet.

It shattered.

They both flinched as the glass exploded in hundreds of pieces on to the carpet. Then they stared at each other. Natasha was appalled by the dark intense understanding in his eyes, and suddenly saw herself as he must see her— nervous, edgy, frightened, strung out like the proverbial cat on a hot tin roof.

The door burst open.

'What the hell was that?' Dolly demanded. 'I thought I——' She stopped, staring at them both, eyes shocked— as well she might be, because only a Martian would not sense the frazzled air of powerful emotion blazing between Natasha and Dominic.

'I knocked a chair over,' Dominic said raggedly, and ran a hand through his tousled black hair. 'I'll pay for the damage, of course.'

'Oh, don't worry about it,' Dolly said. 'A friend of mine will fix the glass for——'

'I insist,' Dominic bit out roughly.

Dolly stared for a second, then said, 'I'm sorry to have disturbed you.' She hesitated, staring at Natasha. 'Are you all right?'

'No, I'm not,' Natasha replied at once, her voice shaking. 'In fact, I think I'll accept your earlier invitation and come to the party with you and Bobby, after all.'

Dominic's dark head swung to stare furiously at her. 'We still haven't gone over the details of your trip to Russia or——'

'I'll look at the papers tomorrow,' she said tightly. 'Please just leave them there and go.'

His mouth tightened. He looked from her to Dolly, then back at her again, and his eyes were jet-black with rage because he knew what she was doing and felt powerless to stop her.

'Fine,' he said harshly, striding towards the door. 'I'll call you tomorrow afternoon to check that you know what you're supposed to be doing.'

'Sweet of you!' she drawled thickly, hating him, and he threw her another black look before striding away down the hall.

The front door slammed behind him.

Dolly looked at her as they both heard his footsteps on the stairs. 'What the hell was all that about?'

'Nothing,' Natasha said thickly, unable to confide in her, for some reason, even though Dolly knew all about Tony, and had never betrayed her confidence, not in all the time she had shared this flat with her. But somehow, the effect Dominic Thorne was having on her was so exceptional that Natasha was afraid to confide in anyone about it.

It's too strong, she realised, horrified.

He's already obliterating Tony from my mind, and the reasons are so numerous I couldn't even list them.

Where Tony had been in his early forties, greying, balding and coldly uncommunicative, Dominic Thorne was thirty-seven, dramatically handsome, sexy, powerful, dynamic, intelligent, sensitive, cynical, gorgeous, rich…

As a man in his own right, Dominic wiped the floor with Tony. But as a man in relation to Natasha, he positively ground Tony out like an old cigar under his expensive, self-assured heel.

And as for her sexual feelings towards Tony—well, she had had none. It had all been platonic, more like play-acting than real love, more like teenage adoration for an unattainable man.

But Natasha knew her sexual feelings for Dominic Thorne were as hot and dangerously hungry as they could get, and if he ever did more than kiss her, she would lose her grip on safety forever.

I've only met him three times, and I'm already emotionally, mentally, sexually and spiritually involved with him. In a big way. More deeply than I ever have been before, and if I don't nip it in the bud, right here and now, I'll end up obsessively, passionately, irrevocably in love with him.

Danger reared like a hissing serpent.
Natasha stepped back in fear from it.
She mustn't feel like that.
Never, ever, ever...

CHAPTER THREE

THE party she attended with Dolly was wonderful fun, but after Dominic's visit, Natasha wasn't really in the mood for fun. In fact, she was unable to think of anything but Dominic.

Sitting on the doorstep of the party house at midnight, she stared into the warm, moonlit sky.

How could he have been so damned clever—and so unfeeling? Even if he had guessed the truth behind her isolated, loveless life, he didn't have to hit her in the face with it, force her to admit to it. It could be argued that he'd just been feeling his way, watching her reactions to see whether he was on the right track or not, but she didn't believe that. Certainly not when she forced herself to sit down and think about why he had done it.

Why? What could he possibly get out of it? Don't tell yourself, she thought fiercely, that he wants to get emotionally involved with you, because that way disaster lies.

Oh, she could just see it now.

Her capacity for limitless passion, undying devotion and supreme love would rear its ugly head again, making her look a fool, be a fool, and cope with the humiliation of obsessive folly, all over again.

Well, I won't go through it, she told herself determinedly. I'd rather die than let a man like Dominic Thorne talk me into getting emotionally involved, just because he finds it a challenge.

46

What other reason could he have, after all? He wasn't in love with her. Nor would he ever be. He just found her an intriguing mystery, as he had so honestly said, and a mystery that he wanted to unravel.

Maybe it was even more basic than that, though, she thought angrily. Maybe it had something to do with that damned stupid reputation she had gained at Thorne Industries, and that would make the challenge for Dominic quite irresistible, and definitely sexually based— to be the man, the one man, who managed to get Natasha Carne into bed.

God, she hated him. How much simpler life would be if he wasn't the very powerful son of her new boss, Xenia Valevsky. After all, no matter what she did from now on, and no matter how hard she tried to avoid Dominic, she was going to run into him.

She ran into him much sooner than she thought.

The very next day, the doorbell rang at one o'clock. Dolly was watching television with Bobby; they were curled up on the couch together like spoons, munching crisps and drinking milk shakes.

Assuming the doorbell had been rung by one of Dolly's friends, Natasha got up cheerfully saying, 'I'll get it...' and walked into the hallway to depress the key on the intercom. 'Hello?'

'Hi, it's Dominic,' drawled the powerful voice that always made her heart skip excited beats. 'Let me in.'

Her mouth tightened and she felt compelled to be cold with him after what he'd done last night, even though she still secretly admired, wanted and adored him.

'There's no need for us to speak, Dominic, let alone meet. I've already gone through the dossier and wallet you left here. I know the flight times, the hotel address, the——'

'Don't be tiresome,' he said tersely. 'I've a duty to check everything is all right. Now come on—let me in.'

She hesitated angrily, then realised that she would look more terrified than cool if she refused, so she pressed the button which opened the downstairs door, and waited in the upstairs doorway, arms folded tightly across her chest, face unsmiling and angry.

Dominic looked gorgeous, as usual, and even sexier today in faded blue jeans and a white shirt which offset his fantastic tan and made his blue eyes seem even more dazzling.

He reached her and towered over her, dwarfing her. 'Hi...'

Natasha glared stonily at him.

'Very welcoming,' he drawled sardonically. 'Look at that face. Medusa in person.'

'Thanks!' she said tightly, eyes flaring at once.

'Well, I've tried the charming approach before, and it didn't work—did it?'

Her lashes flickered in attracted response. 'Approach...?'

'Yes,' he drawled, a smile touching his tough mouth as his eyes glittered over her. 'What do you think I'm doing banging on your door again after the way you behaved last night?'

'The way I behaved!' she flared angrily again. 'My God, that's rich, coming from you! You did everything but browbeat me into telling you very personal secrets about my past!'

'You didn't have to throw me out.'

'What else could I do? You clearly weren't going to stop!'

'Hmm.' He studied her for a second, that smile still touching his mouth, and as his eyes roved over her again he murmured, 'You look stunning, by the way.'

The swift change of tactic and conversation threw her. She just stared at him with her mouth open.

'Very beautiful...' he said softly.

'I thought I looked like Medusa?' she snapped unsteadily.

'Only from the neck up. But I love it when you wear your hair soft and loose. It looks much better.'

'Thank you...'

'And,' he murmured, one long finger touching the neck of her soft green silk wrap top, 'I adore this top. Very silky, very feminine. It's rather exciting to see this secretive sensuality, hidden away from prying eyes, here in the comfort of your home.'

Her face burned and she pushed his finger away from the low neckline of her wrap top, angrily aware that she had shivered with pleasure, and that her nipples had erected under his touch, his gaze.

'Jeans suit you,' he said softly, smiling down at her, eyes admiring the contours of her slender curved body in the green top and faded jeans. 'You look extremely ravishable.'

'I thought you came here to discuss the travel arrangements?' she said icily. 'Again!'

'I lied,' he drawled, lounging against the door-jamb. 'I came to see if I could take you out for the afternoon.'

Her eyes flashed angrily. 'No, you can't!'

'Oh, go on,' he drawled, black lashes flickering charmingly on those rough-hewn cheekbones. 'Let me take you out. It'll really make my day, I promise.'

'I am not interested in making your day.'

He studied her for a second, then said coolly, 'If you refuse, I'll advise my mother not to employ you.'

'That's a cheap shot!'

'Very cheap.' He laughed softly, eyes glittering. 'Despicable. I am a swine, you stand warned.'

Her mouth tightened.

'So, come on,' he drawled. 'What's it to be? An afternoon with your favourite man, or instant dismissal and possible penury?'

'My God, you're a nasty piece of work!' she said furiously, hating him.

'I believe we've already gone through that. Can we move it along a little? I suggest you get your handbag, stick some shoes on, and say bye-bye to Dolly. I'll be waiting outside in the car.' He turned, saying over one broad shoulder, 'It's a white Ferrari, by the way.'

It would be, Natasha thought, detesting him, but she felt her options had been severely limited by his threat and, much as she despised herself for giving in to such obvious and unjust blackmail, she went to her room, got her bag and shoes, then said goodbye to Dolly and Bobby, who were still engrossed in *Casablanca*. Ingrid Bergman had just dissolved into tears rather than shoot Humphrey Bogart. Should have pulled the trigger, thought Natasha furiously. I would, if it was Dominic Thorne.

Outside, the white Ferrari gleamed in the hot afternoon sunlight.

'Fast little mover under pressure, aren't you?' drawled Dominic, as she got into the passenger seat beside him. 'I must remember to threaten you more often.'

She slammed the door, hating him. 'Where, precisely, are we going?'

'For a Sunday afternoon drive.' He flared the powerful engine, a smile on his tough mouth. 'And while we drive, we can talk.'

'I don't want to talk to you,' she said tightly.

'I can always think of more threats, you know,' he drawled, pulling away into the centre of the road and avoiding all the cars parked on either side, glittering in the sun, several men stripped to the waist washing their cars at odd intervals as they sped along, attracting admiring glances at the white Ferrari.

They drove for a while in silence, along the main road, down into West London, past Harrods, which was closed and dark, the Old Brompton Road silent, deserted as always on a quiet Sunday afternoon.

'Did you enjoy your party last night?' Dominic asked coolly.

'Yes.'

'Meet any attractive men?'

Her eyes flared with the desire to provoke. 'Hundreds! And I got all their names and addresses, too.'

He laughed softly. 'Planning on sending them Christmas cards, are you? If I know you, they won't be getting anything more exciting than that.'

'But you don't know me, do you?' she said through her teeth.

'I'm trying to remedy that.'

She breathed erratically, hating him. 'I don't know why—you're just wasting your time.'

'It's my time. I can do what I like with it.'

They drove on in silence, Natasha sitting stiffly in the front seat with her arms folded while Dominic relaxed at the wheel, the warm breeze flickering his dark hair back from his strong forehead.

The car sped along Piccadilly, past the Ritz, past Hatchards, down to the Circus, shabbily alive with young people clustering around the gleaming statue of Eros.

'*Why* are you prepared to waste your time trying to get to know me?' Natasha asked eventually as they headed down the Haymarket. 'I mean—why? What can you possibly hope to get out of all this?'

'The truth.'

She looked away, eyes angry. 'I don't know what you mean by that.'

'OK, well, let's play it another way, shall we?' he drawled coolly, the warm breeze from the open window flickering through his dark hair. 'I want you to answer the question for me. What do *you* think I hope to get out of all this?'

'What!' Natasha glared at him contemptuously.

'Tell me what you think I want.'

She hesitated, aware of the dangers of answering, but she knew he would just keep on at her until she answered, so she tried to remain cool while she thought of a good way to phrase her feelings.

'I'm not sure of everything you might want,' she said eventually. 'But I imagine sex has something to do with it.'

'And what else?'

'Entertainment? I can only imagine you're bored with all your society beauties.' Her eyes flashed. 'Most men would give their eye-teeth to have your selection of models and movie stars, but then, you're probably jaded after years of effortless conquest!'

'How flattering,' he drawled, laughing softly. 'And what else?'

Her mouth tightened. 'You'd like to see me lose my temper again. You obviously enjoyed my behaviour in the office that day, and came round last night to try and provoke another scene like that.'

'Why should I do that?'

'To get some perverse emotional kick out of it!' she said thickly, heart twisting with pain.

'And where might that lead?'

'To me falling wildly in love with you—you hope!' she blurted out furiously. 'So you can stand back and enjoy watching me make a fool of myself over you!'

'Yes, and that's very much to the point,' he shot back. 'That's what you're really afraid of, as we discovered last night. Emotion, feelings, falling in love—and making a fool of yourself.'

'Everyone's afraid of making a fool of themselves!'

'Is that what happened back in Kent?'

Her temper flared as he pressed that old wound. 'Look, I don't have to get involved with men if I don't want to. I'm just a young woman, minding her own business, living her own life, not behaving like a demented rabbit and leaping into bed with every man who happens to pass by!'

'Rabbits don't bother with beds,' he drawled sardonically. 'They just do what comes naturally. And that again is very much to the point, don't you think?'

She looked away, angry eyes staring at Parliament Square as they sped past it, Big Ben glittering in the sunlight, the walls of the Houses of Parliament gleaming cool white stone beyond the green.

'You're not doing what comes naturally, are you, Natasha?'

'I am doing,' she said tightly, 'what comes naturally to me.'

'At this point in your life, sure. But what about the future? Don't you want to fall in love, make love, feel love?'

She said nothing, hating him, glaring stonily out as they turned left and sped along the Embankment.

'Natasha,' he said coolly, 'apart from any consideration of love, you're denying your body what it needs.'

She laughed angrily. 'And I suppose you're the man to put that right, are you?'

'I might be. But I'll bet you a million dollars in used notes that I won't get you anywhere near a bed until I've found out precisely what hurt you in the past.'

A lump formed in her throat. Suddenly, this wasn't so easy to cope with. He really seemed determined to probe into the most painful areas of her past, and she couldn't bear to let him, couldn't bear a man like him, a man she basically admired, liked and respected, couldn't bear him to know what had happened to her.

'Well,' she said, when she had swallowed the lump of emotion in her throat, 'as I don't want to end up in bed with you, I'm hardly likely to tell you what happened in the past.'

'Maybe not right now,' he drawled sardonically, 'but I assure you that some day soon you will.'

The car swept past Cleopatra's Needle, and soon they were in the underpass, heading towards the Tower of London and the gateway to the East End of London.

It naturally did not occur to Natasha that Dominic would drive across that invisible border separating the City from the East End, but he did, and as they headed past Whitechapel station, she began to feel uneasy.

'Why are we in the East End?' she asked.

'No particular reason,' he murmured, but the gleam in his eyes disturbed her.

Soon, they were slowing at a junction which was all too familiar.

She couldn't believe he'd do it, but he did.

He turned off and headed for the M2 to Dover.

'We're going to Kent?' she said fiercely, staring at the familiar stretch of road. 'Is that what you're up to? Is that what all this has been about, you swine?'

'Why shouldn't we drive to Kent?' he drawled sardonically. 'Surely you're delighted? After all, it is your home county, and you do have fond memories of it, don't you?'

She looked at him, eyes fierce green. 'Turn this car round!'

'On a motorway, darling?'

'We're not on the motorway yet!'

'No, but we soon will be. And then we'll be in Kent, and then we'll be—oh, let me think! What *is* the name of that town you used to live in? Could it be...? Could it be Ashford?'

For a long time, she just sat where she was, staring ahead with fury in her eyes, appalled at the thought of going back to Ashford. Just the streets and shops and pubs she would see filled her with a sense of rage, pain and humiliation.

Eventually, she couldn't stay silent any longer, though. She couldn't let him take her back there, and if angry threats wouldn't work, she would have to let her pride go a little.

'Please,' she said, her voice choked with resentment. 'Don't take me back to Ashford.' She looked at him. 'Please, Dominic...'

'Why not?' he asked deeply, his face serious.

She swallowed hard, then said, 'I—I just don't want you to.'

Dominic gave a harsh sigh and carried on driving.

Natasha sat in silence, refusing to give in any more, but she realised as they drove on and on and on that he had every intention of breaking her colossal, fear-born pride one way or the other, and eventually she became too furious with him to keep silent any longer.

'Look,' she said fiercely as they sped on to the motorway, 'why are you doing this? Even if you do take me back to Ashford—what difference will it make to you?'

'I know something's bugging you about the place, and I believe people should always confront what's bothering them, no matter how frightening or painful it is.'

'And where did that belief spring from? I mean—why should it be so very important to you?'

His dark lashes flickered. He said nothing.

'Unless...' Her eyes scanned his handsome face. 'Unless someone hurt *you* in the past, and you had to confront them in order to recover.'

'Everybody gets hurt, Natasha,' he drawled coolly. 'You're not the only casualty of love.'

She couldn't believe a man as gorgeous and desirable as he was would be hurt by any woman, and asked incredulously, 'But who was it?'

'A beautiful, blonde ballerina,' he said expressionlessly, 'called Kyra Kerenskya.'

Of course, she thought, staring—hadn't Xenia told her about Kyra already? That Dominic had once been in love with her, and that Xenia had thought he would end up marrying the beautiful ballerina.

'And what happened?' she asked jealously, unreasonably.

He shot her a cool blue look. 'Now, why should I tell you that when you won't tell me your story?'

Natasha stared for a second, then looked away, frowning. What he said made sense, but of course she was so certain that his pain hadn't been anywhere near as bad as hers that she couldn't possibly confide in him.

After all, he'd had so many women linked to his name, regardless of this fascinating Russian ballerina. There were always stories in the gossip columns about his list of beauties, always photographs of him with this super-model or that movie star or this society beauty.

But Natasha's love-life had been a desert for four years.

'Well, that's enough about me,' Dominic drawled as the car sped along the motorway, great green banks rising sunlit and beautiful on either side. 'Let's talk about you again. And this man who hurt you in Kent. What was his name? Oh yes—I remember. Tony Kerr.'

She gasped, turning to stare.

He laughed at the expression on her face. 'Don't look at me like that. You gave yourself away the day we met—remember? Turning into a banshee and screaming accusations at me, demanding to know if his name had turned up in that report I had done on you.'

Natasha sat rigidly, eyes blazing. 'I see. You've had him checked out too now, have you? My God, you——'

'No, I haven't had him checked out. I thought I'd ask you first. See if you'd tell me your side of the story.'

'But why are you doing this?' she exploded, emotions boiling up in her like wildfire. 'It's none of your damned business!'

'Agreed,' he drawled. 'But you're a very beautiful, desirable woman and I happen to want you.'

'Back to basics, then?' Her voice was raw. 'Back to rabbits and——'

'That's right!' he laughed mockingly. 'Back to bed!'

She turned, seething, and shouted, 'There is no way in hell you are ever going to get me into bed, Dominic!'

'Look at those eyes!' he said softly, inhaling, staring at her. 'And you wonder why I want you! All that tempestuous emotion, four years of pent-up passion, and I want to be the man to get it. My God, I want to take you to bed and detonate you.'

Her breath exhaled in a shaky stream of angry excitement.

'You want it too,' he said softly, glancing at her out of the corner of his eye. 'Don't tell me you don't, because I know just how hard you're fighting me.'

'I'm not fighting you!' she denied thickly.

'Well, if you're not fighting me, sweetie, why are you always so het up in my company?'

'Because you're permanently trying to get at me by digging into my past!'

'I only just started,' he drawled. 'Let's not exaggerate. Oh, look! Speaking of which—there's the turning for Ashford. What fun! I've got your family's address. Why don't we pop in and say hello?'

Natasha breathed erratically, stuck in a nightmare as the car turned off for Ashford and she could only sit helplessly in the front seat of the Ferrari, dreading this confrontation with the past, hating Dominic as the car sped along the country roads towards her nemesis.

'Why, you've gone quite white!' Dominic murmured lazily beside her. 'Not afraid of seeing your charming family again, surely?'

She struggled to keep her breathing even. 'I haven't seen them for four years! I just send Christmas and birthday cards. I have no intention of getting out of the car for a friendly visit!'

'Well, I could always bring them to the car to say hello through the window.'

Natasha tried to hit him.

His hand clamped round her wrist like a metal vice, his face tough as granite and his eyes blazing. 'Don't hit me when I'm driving, you little fool! Do you want us to crash?'

'Get your hands off me, you swine!' she shouted, trying to hit him again.

He slammed on the brakes and screeched to a halt at the side of the road. 'Right!' he bit out, unbuckling his seatbelt with angry hands, eyes blazing as he moved over to her side with dangerous intent. 'I've had just about enough of you, fighting me, lying to me, avoiding all my questions with your——'

'I have every right to do as I please!' she said hoarsely, struggling in panic as he fell on her, took her wrists, pinned them at the sides of her head and crushed her against the seat. 'Stop it, let me go, I can still kick if you——'

'Kick away!' he said thickly, and then his mouth closed over hers, and when she continued to fight, the kiss became bruising, making her cry out as she felt his tongue against hers.

'You're hurting,' she tried to say against his mouth, but he carried on kissing her, and his hand suddenly moved up to cup one full, aching breast, making shivers of angry excitement run through her like hot needles.

A moan of fierce desire came from her mouth.

The kiss changed at once, his mouth coaxing hotly, passionately. She responded, helpless against this, swept away by his touch, his kiss, her mouth opening beneath his in excited response, their tongues and breathing mingling while his hand fondled her breast exquisitely.

'Oh, God...!' Natasha moaned, running her hands over his broad shoulders. 'Don't...don't...!'

He kissed her deeper, his heart thudding hard, and slid his hand down to her hip, down further to her thigh, easing her jean-clad legs apart for him, making her moan even more as the hot onslaught of his mouth combined with the feel of that strong hand moving up her inner thigh, making her whole body burn with sexual hunger.

I can't fight him, she realised dazedly, I want him too much. He was doing wonderfully wicked things to her with his hands and mouth, and she was lost, spreading beneath him, mouth hungry, body arched in passionate response, gasping out loud as she felt that strong hand slip inside her top, inside her bra, to stroke her bare, erect nipple.

'Please...' Her voice was suddenly a humiliated plea. 'Please...'

'Please what?' he said thickly against her swollen mouth, and his long finger stroked her bare nipple exquisitely.

'Please...stop...' she whispered shakingly. 'I can't fight you, I give up, I give in, I admit defeat...'

Dominic broke off the kiss slowly, and raised his dark head to stare down at her flushed, ecstasy-filled face, listening to her hoarse breathing, watching the excited rise and fall of her breasts.

'Darling,' he said softly, 'that's the nicest thing you've ever said to me.'

She flushed deeper, lowered her lashes.

'So...' He was breathing hard too, his eyes very dark. 'I can safely drive on without further trouble from you?'

'For the moment,' she admitted unsteadily, afraid to look at him in direct challenge in case he obliterated her will again with a further onslaught of desire.

Dominic laughed softly and dropped a brief, burning kiss on her lips. 'I suppose it really would be too much to ask for total surrender!'

'I'll never give you that, Dominic!' she agreed huskily.

'Then I'll never fall in love with you, Natasha,' he murmured, and smiled as he watched the dark, obsessive hunger flash suddenly in her hot green eyes.

She lay there staring at him, aware that he was telling her something about life, about love, about men and women, and although she needed to know it, she was afraid, so afraid, so damned terrified of her own capacity for love that she couldn't bear to ask the questions she so desperately needed answers to.

Dominic laughed, and moved back to the driver's seat. 'OK, then. Let's get this show back on the road!'

The engine flared, the car shot away into the traffic, and Natasha struggled to pull herself back together with shaky hands, tidying her tousled hair, smoothing down the green silk top, touching her bruised lips where his hot kiss still lingered temptingly.

As the car sped into Ashford, she asked thickly, 'Are you still going to take me back home like this?'

He inclined his dark head. 'Yes, I am. You see, I really don't think your reasons for cutting off your family are good enough,' he said deeply. 'I think you've let this situation get badly out of hand. You should take this opportunity to drop in, out of the blue, say hello and start mending the bridges.'

Natasha sighed deeply, thinking of her family, as she had done on and off for the last four years, feeling guilty inside at her departure, yet afraid to face them in case they treated her with the same embarrassed pity with which they had treated her four years ago.

'Nothing stays the same,' Dominic said beside her. 'That's the best thing about life. It gives you limitless power to change the things you don't like.'

Her eyes filled with pain. 'What about the things you can't change?'

'Just put them down to fate, and move on.'

'Well, why don't you do that with me? Put me down to fate, move on and leave me alone!'

He laughed under his breath and shot her a lazy blue glance. 'Because I want to make love to you, darling.'

'Well, I don't want to make love to you!'

'Liar,' he said softly, and slid one strong hand on to her thigh.

Her eyes closed with excited pleasure, and he saw that look of dark hunger and smiled.

Then his hand slid off her thigh as he frowned. 'Isn't that your parents' house we just passed?'

'Dominic,' she said, mouth dry as ashes as she stared back at the strange old house, 'I feel sick with nerves about this!'

'Never mind.' He was doing a U-turn, driving back, then slowing at the gateposts. 'It's called Malakova House, isn't it? I remember because of the Russian connection.'

'I don't want to see them!' she said hoarsely, heart thudding.

'Do stop saying that, you're beginning to sound like a broken record.' He stopped the car smoothly and turned to look at her with dark eyes. 'I rather think we're here—don't you?'

CHAPTER FOUR

IT SEEMED so much smaller than she remembered it. The
black wooden gates, the long winding path, bright with
colourful summer flowers, leading to the arched wooden
door surrounded by a trellis of roses. Set back from the
road, the house itself was a strange combination of Tudor
beams and Gothic turrets, an oddity in this Kentish town,
just as the family had always been, just as Natasha had
become.

'Looks rather cute,' Dominic drawled beside her. 'A
little out of place, perhaps, with those turrets.'

'That's why they bought it,' Natasha said huskily,
staring into the past. 'My mother's half Russian, and
my father's half French. They said they specialised in
being a little out of place, so why not be proud of it?'

'Worthy sentiments,' Dominic murmured, smiling. 'I
can't wait to meet them. Come on—let's go.'

Natasha's hand shot out to grip his wrist. 'Please . . . I
don't want to. Not yet.'

'Waiting to get your courage up?' His dark brows
arched. 'The more you wait, the more you'll need. Best
to get it over with. Come on, get out of your own free
will or be carried to the front door by me.'

Natasha sat hating him powerlessly as he got out of
the car and strode round, powerful and charismatic, to
her side. As he opened the door for her she glared at
him, but it was a vulnerable glare, for she was trembling
at the thought of going in there, and praying that nobody
was in.

'I hate you for this!' she told him fiercely as she walked to the gate with him.

'How very exciting of you!' he drawled mockingly, opening the gate. 'I look forward to an extremely stimulating evening tonight, when I get you home. Just think how much fun I'll have when you unleash all that hatred and anger on me.'

The door opened before they reached it.

Her brother Felix stood gaping at her, his jeans and T-shirt loose on his thin, gangly body, a glass of beer in one hand, his dark hair a shaggy mess around his unshaven face.

'I saw the Ferrari,' he said in blank shock. 'I wondered who it was.'

Natasha stared at him, scarcely able to recognise him, for he had changed so much since she'd last seen him four years ago, had shot up from a teenager into a young man, and suddenly she felt waves of love for him, swamping her with a horrified realisation of what she had lost when she walked away from home.

'Natasha?' Felix was staring at her. 'It is you, isn't it?'

'Yes,' she said huskily, quite lost for words.

'And I'm Dominic Thorne,' drawled the powerful man beside her. 'Natasha's boyfriend. The Ferrari's mine, by the way.'

'Wow!' Felix's eyes lit up like a pinball machine and he stared up at Dominic with admiration, then at Natasha with even more admiration. 'Amazing boyfriend you've got!'

'Are your parents at home?' Dominic asked, taking control while Natasha floundered, completely overwhelmed with emotion. 'Perhaps you could tell them that Natasha is——'

'Yes, of course!' Felix turned on his heel and went along the hallway while Dominic took Natasha's arm and led her inside, watching her shocked face with cool blue eyes as he closed the front door behind him.

Excited voices came from the back room. Footsteps, a door thudding, then her mother and father were half running into the hallway, their faces as shocked and delighted as Felix's had been.

It was all terribly tense and emotional.

They all stood staring at each other for one long, tense moment. The grandfather clock ticked into the charged silence.

Her mother Anastasia had aged considerably, her hair more grey than it had been and her pale face more lined, even though the green eyes were still bright. As for her father Michel, his hair had silvered at the temples, making him look very distinguished indeed, still tall and strong, with glittering blue eyes.

'Darling...?' her father whispered, walking to her.

She went into his arms in a flurry of emotion, tears bursting from her eyes, and as he hugged her, kissing her cheek, her mother came to them both and they ended up in a mass of laughter, tears and kisses. Natasha realised in a split second that they had never pitied her, had never been embarrassed by her, but had just been unable to deal with her pain except by giving her privacy.

'Felix, put the kettle on and make some tea.' Anastasia Carne was smiling through her tears, wiping her eyes on a lace handkerchief. 'Come into the lounge, both of you, and tell me everything you've been doing.'

'Dominic won't want tea!' Michel Carne clapped him on the back in a manly sort of way. 'Surely you'd prefer a nice cold beer?'

'Yes, thank you,' drawled Dominic. 'So long as it's just one.'

They went into the lounge in a tumble of excitement, and it was all so different, yet so very much the same.

Natasha stared at the sunlit, flowery couches, the rug on the floor, the little ornaments on the mantelpiece, the painting of her great-grandmother performing in *Swan Lake* at the Kirov hanging above them, the piano in the corner, music piled untidily on top of it, where Felix played obsessively, and the Russian music-box, still in pride of place among the silver-framed photographs on the corner table.

'Oh, look . . .!' Natasha went to the table, touched the music-box, tears of joy in her eyes. 'I can't believe it's still here!'

'It was my grandmother's,' Anastasia said with a tremulous smile. 'I'd never throw it away.'

Natasha opened the black-red lacquered box, and tinny strains of *Swan Lake* echoed in the warm room as the tiny ballerina began to turn in front of the gold-framed miniature mirror.

'That's quite exquisite.' Dominic was standing behind her, his deep voice making her heart leap.

'Her prince gave it to her.' Anastasia came to stand beside them both, smiling. 'It was the only thing of material value she took out of Russia when she fled.'

'That must have been quite a love-story,' Dominic said lazily, turning to smile at Natasha's slender, elegant mother. 'For her to choose a personal treasure to take with her. Most women sewed jewels into their dresses, didn't they?'

Her mother laughed. 'You obviously know a lot about Russian history. Has Natasha been telling you all about our peculiar past?'

'Not at all,' Dominic said softly. 'I'm part Russian myself.'

Her mother and father gasped and exchanged glances.

Natasha lowered her lashes, blushing as she looked away, afraid to think of what was going on in their minds, because all of this was too sudden, too emotional, for her to cope with, and the truth was that she was half inclined to believe Dominic might care for her, might want more than just sex from her.

But if she believed that, she'd get into such dangerous waters, become obsessed with him, fall in love, and end up being brutally hurt, deserted, abandoned.

The ballerina turned softly in the music-box. She thought of her great-grandmother, who had had her grand passion, become pregnant and never married, never stopped loving her prince, even though disaster and revolution had threatened her life, even though he had abandoned her when the child was born, even though she had built a new life for herself... she had never stopped loving her prince.

Clearly, obsessive love ran in the family.

Natasha snapped shut the music-box, turning, green eyes wary.

Dominic looked down at her from his great height, and those heavy eyelids veiled his expression, making her even more wary, because she was beginning to re-alise that he was one step ahead of her, and always had been, ever since she had got into that lift at Thorne Industries and wondered how he knew her name.

'Tea up!' Felix said cheerfully, trundling in with a tea-tray, and they all sat down to enjoy a lazy hour of conversation.

Natasha was very irritated to note that Dominic charmed both her parents and Felix. But she couldn't bring herself to be furious with him, because she was so happy to be home, to be relaxed and at peace with all she had once lost.

Felix played the piano for them while Dominic and her father drank their beer and talked about yesterday afternoon's rugby match.

'And they scored that winning goal,' her father was saying, 'in the last fifteen seconds of the match!'

'That's the way life goes,' drawled Dominic, flicking a mocking look at Natasha. 'Disaster can always turn into success. And it doesn't matter how or when you win—so long as you do it before the final whistle.'

She ignored him, concentrating instead on her mother's talk of her friends, of her bridge parties, her fêtes and charity lunches, and of all the gossip that had gone on in her absence.

'Did I tell you Lizzie Belling had got married for the sixth time?'

'Yes,' Natasha smiled. 'You told me in your last letter.'

'Such a shame.' Her mother touched her hand tentatively. 'That we should only have communicated by post for so long.'

Tears filled Natasha's eyes as she nodded, lost for words.

'Don't leave it so long again, will you, dear?' Her mother looked so sad. 'You know we really do miss you terribly. I know it's your life, and you have a perfect right to do as you please, but try to remember us occasionally. Even if it is only once in a few years.'

Natasha struggled not to burst into tears on the spot again. 'I won't leave it so long again, Mother. I promise.'

Dominic watched her with a cool smile, and when she gave him a tearful look, her mouth trembling beyond control, his blue eyes softened. He glanced at his watch, and drawled, 'Well—I really think it's time we got going. Natasha . . . ?'

'Yes, we must get back to London.' Natasha stood up, her legs rather weak. 'I'm afraid I have to be up early in the morning. I'm going to St Petersburg, remember.'

Her parents and Felix saw her to the door, chattering excitedly about her new job and all it entailed. Natasha agreed to get a signed copy of one of Xenia's books for her mother, who was also a great fan.

They spilled out into the hot afternoon in a shower of kisses and waves and tears. Dominic led her to the white Ferrari, put her inside, and her family stood waving from the front door as they drove away.

'There you are,' Dominic drawled triumphantly as they sped along the main road out of Ashford. 'That wasn't so bad, was it?'

Natasha sniffled like a small child, overwhelmed by the reception she had got from her family, and horrified by the years she had lost. She stared out of the window in thoughtful silence as the car sped back to the motorway, then back to London.

By the time they drove back into the City, the tears were dry on her face, and she was out of the emotional shock Dominic had so relentlessly made her go through.

Sunset gleamed red-gold in the sky, turning Lloyd's into a shimmering firmament of blood-streaked glass and chrome. Black taxis and red buses were moving around the civilised streets, usually so crowded with financial office workers, now so empty on Sunday.

This time tomorrow, she would be in another city— St Petersburg.

Natasha looked at Dominic's hard, handsome profile as he drove, and realised for the first time that her life was changing so fast she could barely keep up with it, and that the changes were inextricably linked with this man.

'Why are you really doing this?' she asked him huskily.

The dark head turned. 'Doing what?'

'You know very well what.' Her voice was dark, calm, serious. 'I haven't had a moment's peace since I met you. You're like a whirlwind, blowing through my life, turning it all upside-down and shaking me till my teeth rattle.'

'Darling,' he drawled sardonically, 'that's the second nicest thing you've ever said to me.'

'Don't hold your breath. It won't happen very often.'

He laughed, and slid a hand on her slender, jean-clad thigh. 'Oh, I don't know about that, Natasha. I think if I play my cards right, you'll say much more exciting things to me in the future.'

Pulses leaping, she wantonly allowed his hand to remain on her thigh, and he more than noticed it, his mouth pursing with obvious desire as he watched her hotly through his lashes.

Soon, they were back at her flat.

'I'm exhausted,' Dominic murmured beside her, his long fingers sliding along her thigh. 'Mind if I come in and have a cup of coffee?'

Breathless, she stared at him with her strange, obsessive green eyes, knowing perfectly well that if she let him come in he would try to make love to her, and knowing also that she wanted him badly, so badly that she could scarcely bring herself to refuse.

Yet she must. She must refuse, and keep on refusing, because he represented grand passion at its most lethal, and she could not allow it to take hold of her.

'I don't think that's a very good idea,' she said thickly.

'Oh, don't you?' he said flatly. 'Well, I do, and I won't have any arguments about it.' He took his hand off her thigh and got out of the car without another word, slamming the door, striding round to her.

Natasha was both angry and secretly thrilled, getting out of the car as he towered menacingly over her, and she was already imagining a kiss, those hard lips moving hotly, passionately over her own...

'Am I ever going to be able to get rid of you?' she demanded contrarily.

'If I ever believe you sincerely want to be rid of me,' he drawled arrogantly, 'you won't see me for dust.'

That sent a shiver of fear through her heart, but she didn't show it, told herself she was pleased at the prospect, and walked up to her front door, unlocking it while praying that Dolly was not at home, because if she was Dominic might not kiss her, and she badly wanted to be kissed.

Her heart was drumming with excitement as she let them both into the upstairs flat.

'Dolly!' she called into the empty silence.

The fridge hummed, her voice echoed in the dusky hall, and Dolly was definitely out.

'Coffee, then?' Dominic murmured above her head.

Her eyes darted up to his, her body was alive with excitement, and as her hot, passionate gaze moved to his mouth, she felt his hands on her slender waist, drawing her towards him.

Their mouths met in slow, mutual hunger, and she let her eyes close, a moan coming from her throat, her arms winding strong and passionate around his neck as he pressed her slender body against his.

He kissed her deeply, drinking from her mouth as she drank from his, their tongues and breathing mingling hotly. His hands moved down to cup her rear, pressing her harder against him until she felt the hot evidence of his own physical excitement against her stomach.

Dizzy with excitement and need, she let her body melt responsively against his and was rewarded with a fierce groan from him, which made her pulses leap higher, and made Dominic press her closer, caressing her buttocks arousingly, making her burn and burn and burn.

'Oh, God...!' he said thickly against her mouth, and then she was floating as he carried her, still kissing her, breaking off to say raggedly, 'Which one is your bedroom?'

'No!' she said hoarsely, dazed and horribly excited. 'We mustn't go into the bedroom or——'

'Never mind, I'll take my chances!' His mouth silenced her protests as he kicked open the nearest door and strode in, as luck would have it, to her bedroom, going direct to the bed, letting the door swing shut as he put her down on the bed, his body covering hers as he joined her.

'Don't!' she said hotly, half with panic, half with excitement.

'Just shut up and let me kiss you!' he bit out thickly in the twilit semi-darkness, and his mouth burned down over hers with insatiable need as his breathing quickened, his heartbeat thundered, and his flushed face almost burnt her skin.

Natasha couldn't fight her own desire, let alone his, so she found herself drowning in pleasure for the first time in her life, cries of hoarse, shaking excitement coming from her as she felt his long fingers slide open the green silk wrap, push it slowly apart, then start to bare her breasts, freeing them from the lacy bra.

'Oh, God!' she whispered fiercely. 'Oh, Dominic, Dominic...!' His hands were cupping her bare breasts, stroking the painfully erect nipples, and she responded like a woman driven mad with pent-up longing, twisting restlessly beneath him, her mouth passionate and hungry against his, her legs splaying as one long hard thigh pushed firmly between them.

He let the wrap top slide to the floor, his fingers deft as he unhooked the lace bra, kissing her wildly, stripping her naked to the waist, running his shaking hands over her body, her stomach, her ribcage, her full, aching breasts.

Natasha moaned in fevered response, blind to all thought now, driven only by the intense desire that had raged between them since they had met, and which now was being unleashed, let out, to rise up in towering intensity between them.

She felt herself begin to touch him, gasps of pleasure coming from her as she unbuttoned his white shirt with shaking fingers, pushed it ruthlessly from his shoulders, threw it to the floor, let her hands move over his broad chest, electrified by the feel of that hot skin, the black hairs and the heartbeat which thundered violently beneath her fingers.

'I want you!' he said thickly, and ran one firm hand along her spread thigh. 'Oh, God, I want you so much I can barely think!' His mouth crushed hers hungrily, his hand moving higher and higher, and when he cupped the soft mound between her thighs they both let out shaking cries of mutual excitement.

Dominic breathed harshly, face darkly flushed as his hands fumbled with the zipper of her jeans.

'No!' Her hand stopped him as common sense came rushing back at her, not overriding her desire—if anything, inflaming it—yet she had to stop him, she couldn't let him take her so easily, no matter how desperately she wanted this never-before-tasted forbidden fruit. 'No, Dominic! No!'

He stared down at her with eyes like molten blue fire. 'You want this as much as I do, Natasha. Let me take you. I won't hurt you, I——'

'No, Dominic!' she blurted out in passionate panic. 'You must know I can't let this happen!'

'Why not?'

'Because we barely know each other!' Her green eyes flared with fear and love and hate. 'This is much too fast for me! I don't like being swept away with passionate frenzy like this, it's——'

'Passionate frenzy?' His mouth burned down over hers, his hands swept up to fondle her bare breasts, stroking the nipples while she moaned in despairing excitement. 'Is that how you feel, Natasha?' His mouth wrenched an inch from hers as he breathed thickly. 'It's how I feel, too. You're not alone. I've wanted you since I first saw you, and I've thought of nothing but you since then. Nothing but you—and this...' His powerful chest gently crushed hers, and the feel of skin on skin was like water to a starving woman, making her head spin as her thighs slid softly apart again, her hips pressing up in instinctively provocative movements against the hard jut of his body.

Suddenly, all she could think of was letting him undress her, undress himself, slide naked between her legs to take her, enter her, detonate her with pleasure.

Danger threatened.

Terror rose up in her.

She pushed at him, and when he refused to stop kissing her, touching her, she began to fight in deadly earnest, her face like a wildcat's, all green eyes and bared teeth, red hair a storm on the pillow as her hands flew and scratched and fought for freedom.

'For God's sake!' he shouted hoarsely, gripping her wrists, pinning them to the bed, staring down at her, a long red cut running across his rough-hewn cheekbone. 'What the hell do you think you're doing!'

'Stopping you!' she flung fiercely. 'Stopping this! I told you I didn't want to do it, and you refused to stop! What was I supposed to do—just lie back and think of Russia?'

'You do want to do it, though,' he bit out thickly. 'You want it so badly I can almost see the steam rising from your skin.'

'I'm an adult woman,' she said tightly. 'I can deny myself anything I want—including you—and nobody can condemn me for it!'

'Oh, sure!' His eyes were angry. 'Left to your own devices, you'll go on denying yourself everything on the list. Let's write it all down and see how you're punishing yourself. No love, no family, no sex, no——'

'The way I live my life is my business!'

'Not any more it's not!' he bit back furiously. 'I've decided to make it my business, and there's precious little you can do to stop me.'

'I can refuse to see you again!' she said hoarsely, mouth shaking as she realised the extent of his determination. 'I can refuse to go to Russia tomorrow, I can refuse to take the job with your mother, I can——'

'Do it, then!' he snarled. 'I'll follow you. I'll hunt you down like the terrified little doe you've turned yourself into, and I'll pick you off in my sights. A fate you richly deserve, given your unbelievable cowardice.'

Tears sprang to her eyes, tears of rage and hatred. 'I am not a coward!'

'Yes, you are!' he said contemptuously, and released her with an angry shove, making her catch her breath with emotional pain as he got off the bed, towering over her, hands thrust in the pockets of his jeans, bare chest magnificent in the half-light. 'God knows why I even want you at all! Look at the way I'm having to bully you, every step of the way, into picking up the pieces, letting go of the past and getting on with your life!'

She flinched on the bed, naked to the waist, her green eyes vulnerable and her red hair streaming down her slender back.

'Well, I've started doing it now, and I'm not giving up.' His mouth bit the words out like a steel trap as he leant over her, face threatening. 'Do you understand me? I'm going to get you into bed and make you mine, no matter what I have to do. So please feel free to run away to Outer Mongolia without leaving a forwarding address, because I warn you, I will find you, and when I do, I will have what I want!'

Fear struck at her heart, because she could see he meant it, and she knew without a shadow of doubt now that if he ever succeeded, if he ever made fierce, passionate love to her as he so nearly had just now, she would be lost forever in the very deepest cauldron of obsessive love.

And she had never experienced her capacity for obsession at its worst, because she had never made love with a man, not even gone beyond a kiss before.

Now that Dominic had taken her past the first few barriers with this passionate lovemaking, Natasha knew with terrifying certainty that he was *the one*—he held the power ultimately to destroy her.

If he ever made love to her, she would find her nemesis in him, the grand passion she had been desperate to avoid all her life...

'Yes, that's right,' he drawled thickly, eyes blazing. 'Look at me like that and realise that I mean every word I say. At least that way I can be sure you know what you're up against in me.'

'I already know,' she whispered hoarsely as she shivered. 'But I'm not completely powerless, Dominic. I can find a way to fight back.

His eyes narrowed menacingly. 'Such as?'

'Another man?' she suggested softly, wanting to hurt him.

He studied her for a second, his teeth bared.

Suddenly, she was flung back on the bed, landing with a gasp to find his hands biting into her bare shoulders, his face inches from hers, fierce blue rage in his eyes.

'You take another man to your bed,' he bit out harshly, 'and I'll snatch you, bundle you off to a secret address, and treat you as a harem slave until you beg me for your freedom.'

'I'll beg you now!' she whispered passionately, excited by his words, her heart hammering while she struggled to retain her common sense. 'I'll beg you now, Dominic!'

He smiled suddenly, his eyes glittering, and bent his dark head to kiss her hot throat, making her gasp in appalled pleasure as his mouth moved lower, taking one hard nipple between tongue and teeth, rolling it as she moaned out loud, her head going back in exquisite delirium.

'You see?' he said thickly, raising his head to look at her. 'You do want me. Admit it.'

Natasha stared passionately at him through her eye-lashes and said, 'I don't deny that I want you. I just deny that I'll let you take me.'

He straightened suddenly, eyes narrowing. 'Then I'll have to find a way to force your hand.'

'There is no way.' She sat up, proud suddenly of her nakedness, unaware of her magnificence in the tight blue jeans, her red hair streaming down her slender back, full breasts flushed with arousal. 'There's not a thing you can do to make me change my mind and go to bed with you!'

His eyes gleamed and he said softly, 'I can get a de-tailed report on Tony Kerr.'

Natasha's face turned white as porcelain, her mouth taut as she said fiercely, 'You dare!'

He laughed, bending to pick up his shirt from the floor.

'You dare, Dominic, and you will *never* get me into a bedroom, let alone a bed!'

'Oh, I don't know about that,' he drawled, shrugging into his shirt. 'After all, he seems to be my biggest stum-bling-block, and I hate stumbling-blocks. They make me want to kick them out of the way.'

Natasha got off the bed, eyes blazing. 'If you get a report on Tony or anything that happened between us, I'll kill you!'

'How very passionate of you!'

'I mean it, Dominic!'

'Well, you know how to stop me.' He buttoned his shirt up with long fingers. 'Just tell me the whole story yourself.'

She looked away, mouth bleached white, appalled at the thought of either possibility. It would be horrific for him to get a detailed report on Tony, but however much she wanted to stop him, she couldn't bring herself to tell him the truth herself. It was too damned humiliating and, no matter what else had passed between Dominic and herself, she felt very sure that she had so far kept his respect. He would lose it if he found out how obsessive she had been about Tony. He would despise her, just as everyone else had done. The limitless capacity she had for passionate love would make her look ridiculous in his eyes, and although her family had clearly forgiven her long ago, that was only because blood was thicker than water. Dominic wasn't related to her. He wouldn't forgive and understand and forget. He would just laugh, then walk away from her.

He stood watching her, dressed now, hands on hips, face arrogant. 'Well?'

'Well, what? Will I tell you all the gory details of my affair with Tony Kerr?' Her eyes blazed with fierce pride. 'I'd rather stick a knife in my own heart than ever tell you anything about that!'

'But the way won't be clear for me,' he said coolly, 'until you do.'

Natasha looked away angrily.

'Or any man, for that matter.'

'I told you—I don't want a man!'

'Not much!' His hands caught her naked shoulders, pulled her against him, made her gasp with pleasure as her bare breasts made contact with him and she felt his hands slide down her naked spine. 'Want me to put you back on the bed and remind you just how much you *do* want a man?'

She tried to wrench away, her face flushed with excitement, and he laughed at her, slid one strong hand up to cup her bare breast, making her give a hoarse moan of muffled desire, her eyes flickering half closed.

His dark head bent, his mouth ravaged her shivering throat, and she moaned again as she pushed him angrily away.

'Don't!' Her heart was banging fiercely with excitement, she wanted him to make love to her, she wanted to drown in his eyes, in his body, in his love, but she was afraid, too afraid, and her only hope was to keep pushing him away, no matter how much she wanted him. 'I don't want you to touch me again like that!'

'Such a coward, Natasha!' he bit out thickly, staring down at her with angry desire. 'You'd rather bury yourself for the rest of your life than face up to the truth—that you stopped living the day that man hurt you, and you're too scared to try and start again.'

'That's my problem!' she said fiercely, covering her breasts with her hands and hating him.

'No, it's mine. Because I want you far too much to let you slither away into your private sarcophagus like some heart-broken Egyptian queen, pining for the man that got away, when you could have a real-life flesh and blood man instead—me!'

'I am not pining for him!' she shouted, eyes blazing. 'I stopped loving that swine four years ago, and I haven't loved him since! I just don't want to get involved again— not the way I was with him! Can't you understand that?'

'Why? How were you involved with him? What was wrong with the way you felt?'

She hesitated, too afraid even to tell him that.

'OK,' he said tightly. 'Have it your own way. I'll put my agency on to his tail tomorrow and they'll be investigating before you even land in St Petersburg!' He turned on his heel, face set with determination, and strode to the door.

Natasha heard the slam of the front door moments later, and she did consider running after him, but she knew now there was no point—he meant to do as he said.

Struggling into her green silk wrap top, she ran into the living-room and looked out of the window in time to see the white Ferrari roaring away into the night, red tail-lights flashing.

A power-driven car, she thought, for a power-driven man. It was what he wanted, wasn't it? To have power over her: not just sexual, but emotional power as well. Why else would he be so determined to find out what had happened with Tony?

Sinking down on to the couch, she tried to think.

If she resigned from her new job as Xenia Valevsky's secretary, she would be out in the job market again, and while she didn't mind that so much, she would have to go to Dominic at some point to get a reference. Ted Leachman, fired himself, would hardly give a reference, and if he did it would probably be vicious. At this stage of the game, it would make life extremely difficult for her to resign. Better to wait until Xenia herself was in a position to give her a reference.

But how long would she have to stay in Xenia's employ before she could conceivably resign and get a good reference? Without one, her chances of getting an equal job were slim. Especially with a six-month gap and sudden resignation from Thorne Industries.

So resigning was hardly the intelligent strategic manoeuvre.

No, she would have to carry on as planned, fly to St Petersburg in the morning, and hope that her next encounter with Dominic was a very long way in the future.

But even if it was, by the time they met again he would have a file on her and Tony Kerr twenty inches thick, and he would have all the information he needed to get her measure completely.

He would know that she was a virgin, and she knew what that would tell him.

That all her pent-up passion was just waiting for the right man to come along, sweep her off her feet, make wild love to her—and reap the rewards of her savagely obsessive heart.

Her eyes closed in horror. Would he track down Tony himself and get all the gory details? How she had fallen heavily in love with him after a brief, platonic three-month relationship? How she had refused to let him go. How she had followed him around town, turning up at his house, his office, sending him letters, cards, ringing him constantly...

Like a teenager with a crush on her idol, she had adored him, worshipped him—and all without sexual involvement.

Oh, God, it was so humiliating, like living through it all again, watching helplessly from the sidelines as she made a complete and utter fool of herself with misdirected passion.

It wasn't my fault! she thought fiercely, hating Dominic for dredging it all up again. I genuinely thought Tony loved me, and he deliberately made me believe our friendship was over because I'd done something wrong. I believed that if I put it right, if I convinced him I loved him, that everything would be fine again, he would love me again, just as he used to...

But of course, that hadn't been the case at all.

Natasha hadn't done anything wrong. Tony had just wanted to end the relationship, and hadn't had the

courage to tell her he was bored with her slavish adoration, especially as he so clearly did not want ever to
make love to her, or even kiss her properly. Instead, he
had told her he didn't want to make love to her because
he respected her too much. And then, when he ended
it, he had told her he had been hurt by her, couldn't
trust her again, and felt bitter because she hadn't loved
him enough.

Why else would she have chased him so feverishly?

Why? she thought in horror.

Because I'm obsessive, capable of raging passions,
undying devotion, all-consuming desire and relentless
love.

No matter what she blamed on Tony, she could hardly
deny the truth about herself. He couldn't have made her
chase him like that if it hadn't been in her to do it. He
probably didn't mean her to respond as she had. He just
happened to be the man who pressed all the right buttons
in her foolish young heart, and unleashed a tempestuous
woman from the chains of civilised behaviour which
bound her.

And now it's on the cards again, she thought in
despair.

Dominic was pressing all the right buttons and more.

Dominic was making her bedroom switchboard light
up like a pinball machine, complete with alarm bells and
sirens and flashing red lights. He was getting to her in
a way that no man ever had—not even Tony. He was
going to obliterate Tony from her memory and punch
his own way through to possess her totally, utterly.

She could feel her resolve beginning to weaken, could
feel her emotions honing in on him, getting lined up with
him in their sights, like a megawatt laser beam ready to
focus on one man.

It had been building since she had first met him, but she had thought she'd be able to resist.

Until today, when he made love to her and she practically exploded with pent-up desire, moving against him uninhibitedly, tearing his clothes off, wishing all hers could go too, and that he would do as he said he wanted to—detonate her.

But did he really want her to be detonated? Did he have any idea of the depths of passion which she was capable of? Or would he reject her in contemptuous horror when he finally succeeded in unleashing her?

He had worked hard to get this far—chasing her, pushing at her, prying into her past, insisting she go back to visit her family...

And she was so grateful that he had done that. If anything, it made her love him, because he had healed a terrible rift there, and healed it with kindness, understanding, patience. She had truly believed that her parents were embarrassed by her, but today had shown her clearly that she was mistaken. They obviously understood how deep her passions ran. In fact, her mother had often told her how like her great-grandmother she was, not only in looks but in temperament.

But that was scary, wasn't it?

To be like her great-grandmother, that bewitching redhead with fiery green eyes who had danced for tsars and grand dukes at the Kirov, and who had fallen heavily, deeply, obsessively in love with a prince...

Natasha was lucky that her love for Tony Kerr had not lasted for eternity, as her great-grandmother's had for her prince. She was aware that Tony had merely tapped into the wealth of emotion she had—the truth was that she had never really loved him, not really, or she would not now be recognising the depths of the all-consuming emotional, spiritual and sexual love that Dominic was going to get from her.

Oh, yes, she thought in passionate terror, I could love Dominic Thorne.

For he is as fiery, determined and emotional as I am...

CHAPTER FIVE

ST PETERSBURG gleamed in the afternoon sun, a city of golden spires and dreaming canals, palaces rising along the banks of the Neva river where Peter the Great first built his ravishing vision to rival Paris, Venice and Amsterdam put together. He had been a mighty tsar, an exceptional man, and they said he had built this city on the bones and blood of a thousand Russians...

Natasha sat in the back of the limousine, staring out at the city she had dreamt of seeing all her life, and thought of Russian history at every turn of the wheels.

There was the gold spire of the St Peter and Paul fortress, where every tsar since Peter was buried, and which the mob had stormed on the day revolution broke out. It shone like a beacon, far across the blue waters of the Neva, piercing the sunlit sky.

There was the Winter Palace, sea-green and white, statues lining its walls, pillars guarding each entrance, and as the car turned to drive past the square, the black marble column in the cobbled centre rose up, a gold angel glittering on top of it, holding a golden cross.

Her heart beat fast with excitement, imagining life as it had been a century ago, when beautiful women in diamonds and furs had driven in troikas across the snow-packed bridges and canals to meet their lovers or attend balls at the Winter Palace.

It must have been such a wonderful, romantic city then, before the tragedies, before the bloodshed. Hundreds of peasants had been shot dead in this very square, right in front of the Winter Palace, on Bloody Sunday, and that single act of brutality had led directly, over ten long, bitter years, to the revolution which ended imperial Russia forever.

'It must be wonderful for you.' Xenia's voice broke into her thoughts. 'To see it all for the first time.'

'It's a dream come true.' Natasha watched the palace square disappear around the corner. 'And the combination of Communist and imperial buildings is quite strikingly bizarre, but beautiful. I wonder what it was like when my great-grandmother was alive?'

'Where did she live?' Xenia asked suddenly beside her.

'Close to Kchessinska's mansion.' Natasha turned to look at her. 'I don't know where that is, but I know she was friendly with Kchessinska.'

'But of course she would have been.' Xenia smiled. 'Mathilde Kchessinska was a prima ballerina and mistress to the tsar before his marriage. I'm sure the two were very good friends. I'll show you her mansion while we're here.'

'Is it still standing?' Natasha asked.

'The mob ransacked it on the day of the revolution, but it's been preserved, not far from here.'

The car turned a corner, and Natasha smiled at the sight of St Isaac's Cathedral, fresh and alive, no longer just a photograph in her mind, the gold dome dazzling in the sunlight, long golden pillars on dusty stone steps, and opposite it, far across the manicured lawns and flowers of the square, the Mereyensky Palace.

'Oh, the Mereyensky Palace! My great-grandmother danced there, in the Kirov!'

'I shall ask Dominic to take you there one evening while he's here.'

Natasha caught her breath, heart thudding violently. 'Dominic? He's coming here? To St Petersburg?'

'Yes, didn't he tell you?'

'No!' Her stomach churned with angry excitement. 'He did not tell me!'

'How very odd.' Xenia frowned, studying her as the car sped through the crowded, crumbling, sunlit streets. 'He said he dropped in to see you yesterday. I felt sure he would have——'

'When is he planning to come?' she asked thickly, struggling to maintain a calm façade.

'I'm not sure, and nor is he. When he can get away, he says, which could mean any time.' Xenia laughed softly. 'He's such a driven man, my son! Always flying around the world buying companies, branching out, making deals, making money...'

Making trouble, thought Natasha, her face pale and her eyes hectic. He was going to come here, was he? When he could get away? Well, she didn't have to be a genius to understand what that meant.

As soon as that report on Tony came through, he'd be on a plane to Russia, and no matter what she did, she wouldn't be able to escape either him or his determination to pry so deeply into her past that he pried her right into bed.

I must stop him doing it, she thought fiercely. I must make sure he never gets me alone, never gets me into a whirlwind of emotion, never provokes me into a display as passionate as the one he provoked last night at my flat.

He only managed to do that by putting her through such a powerful emotional trauma first, of course. Taking her down to see her parents, heal the rift and smooth away all her fears of rejection from them had been a very clever move. She could hardly believe he'd done it out of genuine love for her.

At least, she mustn't believe he had done it out of love. That was too dangerous. It would unleash the demon inside, let her out of those self-imposed chains and free her to run into Dominic's arms, crying out her love, tearing off her clothes, making wild love with him, letting herself be free, free, free . . .

Her nails dug deep into the palms of her hands in an effort to keep control of that passionate woman inside, the woman she had locked up for so many years, not allowing her air or life or self-expression because she was too afraid of the consequences.

And she was still afraid, terribly afraid, of how deeply her feelings for Dominic would grow if he came to her and made love to her while she was in this hothouse of emotion, Russia.

Then he really will detonate me, she thought, shuddering with fear and excitement.

'Here we are, dear,' Xenia said beside her, and she looked up, startled out of her intense thoughts.

The Hotel Europe gleamed in imperial splendour, making Natasha catch her breath with a new kind of excitement at the thought of staying here for two whole weeks.

'I'm quite exhausted,' Xenia said as they entered the hushed, fabled portals of that fabulous hotel. 'I think I shall take a bath, a nap, and then some tea. Please feel free to entertain yourself this afternoon.'

Natasha stared around in awe at the stunning green marble pillars, hallway, chandeliers, palms and uniformed staff. It was simply too beautiful to believe.

They took the lift up, a porter brought their cases, and Natasha's eyes widened even further as she saw the

enormous suite she was sharing with Xenia. It was bigger
than her flat. There were two luxurious living-rooms, a
dining-room, two double bedrooms, and two *en suite*
bathrooms with baths in them big enough for six people.

Xenia went off to take a bath, leaving her alone in an
exquisite living-room.

Natasha moved slowly to the open French windows,
the long lace curtains blowing gently in the summer
afternoon breeze, and looked out at the city of her
childhood dreams, the city of a lost era, the capital city
of imperial Russia long, long ago.

Again, she felt that brush with change...

As though the summer breeze whispered secrets as it
touched her hair, her skin, as though she was meant to
be here, and it would change her life forever.

Her life had stood still for four years, four long, calm,
stable years. But the day she had got into that lift and
seen Dominic running towards her, everything had begun
to change, as though time was moving forwards after a
long, intolerable hiatus.

It was all so personal.

And it was all connected with Dominic.

For it wasn't just a new job he had given her, but a
fairy-tale city she had dreamt of since she was a little
girl, and here she stood, at twenty-six, looking out at
the golden spires of St Petersburg because of one man—
Dominic Thorne.

Natasha had once had a book in which was a photograph of a broken angel, underneath which were in-
scribed the words: 'My life is like a broken stair, winding
round and leading...nowhere.'

That was a perfect description of her emotional life
until she had met Dominic. Now, here she was, flung in
at the deep end, having to cope with the passionate

emotional rush she felt for St Petersburg as well as that
maddening, gorgeous, sexy, driven, powerful, dangerous
man...Dominic.

Would he really come out here to see her?

God help me if he does, she thought.

And God help me if he doesn't.

The next day, she and Xenia began work in earnest.

Natasha had already read the synopsis of Xenia's new
book, and was thrilled to discover that it was being set
at the exact period when her great-grandmother had been
alive and living here.

'I'm basing the family,' Xenia told her over breakfast,
'on the Yusopovs. I take it you've heard of them?'

Natasha smiled. 'The Yusopovs were the richest family
in all the Russias.'

'Is that all you know?'

'Their ancestors had whispered into the ears of the
tsars since the time of Peter the Great,' she said with
high drama, laughing. 'They had diamond mines and
oil fields and one of the Yusopovs gave to his wife for
her birthday a small mountain in the Crimea. Shall I go
on?'

Xenia smiled, arching fine brows. 'Do you know anything about Prince Felix Yusopov?'

'He killed Rasputin in the basement of the Moika
Palace in December 1916,' Natasha went on, eyes glittering obsessively. 'He poisoned him with cyanide, shot
him three times, and finally tied him up, dumped him
into the frozen Neva, and left him to drown.'

'I can see you know your stuff.'

'I've always been fascinated by Russian history, as I
told you. I must have read every book I could lay my
hands on.'

'You obsessive little thing!'

Natasha's face froze, a darkness burning in her eyes
as she heard that fearful word spinning round and round
in her mind and wanted to deny it, shy away from it,
fight it in her own nature.

For the next few days, she was washed away on a tide
of glittering imperial beauty as they visited palace after
palace, including the fabled Hermitage, built by
Catherine the Great and part of the Winter Palace, where
the walls were literally papered with masterpieces from
all over the world, and the French Impressionists incited
gasps of delight as Natasha reeled from Van Gogh to
Matisse, from Cézanne to Gaugin, from Monet to
Manet, from Renoir to Rousseau...

The Winter Palace itself was a miracle, the great
staircase gleaming with gold and grey marble pillars,
chandeliers swaying softly in vast ceilings, and the imperial carriage a stunning gold-encrusted piece of extravagance worthy of revolutionary fury.

They whirled from one beautiful place to the next,
seeing the marble tombs of the tsars at the fortress of
Peter and Paul, the gold icons covering the walls of St
Isaac's Cathedral, the pale blue beauty of Smolny
Cathedral, and always coming back to that central blue
river, the river of Peter the Great's vision, the Neva.

On Thursday evening, the telephone in their suite rang,
just as Natasha was massaging her weary feet.

Xenia was in the bath, so she answered it, surrounded
by shopping bags filled with souvenirs: matryoshka dolls,
icons, scarves, guide-books and little statuettes.

'*Da*?' she said in Russian, expecting it to be a business
call.

'Natasha?' Dominic's deep, dark, gorgeous voice made
her head spin.

For a second she was too breathless to speak, her heart racing as her eyes flared dark, passionate green with the sudden influx of emotion he was now so capable of invoking in her, like Satan in one of his disciples.

'Natasha?' His voice lowered to a dark, intimate level. 'I know it's you—don't try to deny it.'

'Clever of you, darling,' she said flippantly, but her tone was as dark and intimate as his and they both knew it. 'I'm so flattered you recognised my voice. But then, it's hardly surprising, given that I'm clearly not your mother!'

'No, my mother would be pleased that I called.'

'She obviously doesn't know what you're really like.'

He laughed softly. 'Sticks and stones, darling. How are you enjoying St Petersburg?'

'How do you think?'' Natasha sank back down slowly on to the couch, feeling pulled into another world, just by the sound of his voice, and the intensity of feeling he invoked. 'I've dreamt of seeing it all my life. I feel as though I've landed in fairyland, only it's actually real.'

'Have you thought about your great-grandmother at all?'

'Of course.'

'Exceptional woman,' he drawled, as though he had known her personally. 'Lived an exceptional life, too. All that passion and devotion to her prince, even after he left her, even after she fled the country, even on her deathbed.'

'Yes . . .'

'Capable,' he said softly, 'of obsessive love.'

Her breath caught and she couldn't reply, felt herself stiffen, saw his dark mocking face in her mind and knew that he knew, knew that he had found out all about her, knew that he had every detail in that damned report, and that he planned to use it against her.

'I have an old sepia photograph of her in my hand,' Dominic's voice murmured across the miles of Europe which separated them. 'Has anyone ever told you that you look just like her?'

'Shut up, Dominic!' she whispered fiercely, hating him.

'You are like her, aren't you, Natasha?' he went on softly. 'Both in looks and temperament. I should have known the minute I met you. All that seething emotion, all that blazing passion, just waiting to get out like a genie from a bottle——'

'Shut up!' She was on her feet suddenly, heart thumping with fear.

'Like a woman wailing for her demon lover.'

'I told you to shut up!'

He laughed softly. 'I always loved that line from "Kubla Khan". I wanted to be a demon lover, you see, but I needed the kind of woman who could cope, and I can't help thinking I've found her in you.'

'But I can't cope!' she said fiercely.

'Perhaps not,' he drawled, 'but I want to experience lovemaking with a woman of your extreme passions, and I'll enjoy proving that to you, forcibly, when I arrive in St Petersburg tomorrow afternoon.'

'Tomorrow!'

'I'll be with you by three. Look forward to it, darling...' he drawled mockingly, and then the line went dead as he hung up with a cool click that made her want to fly down the line in dark avenging spirit to scream at him.

For a long time, she just stood there, clutching the receiver in a damp hand, her heart drumming with fear and excitement, picturing him striding in here tomorrow, that powerful face, those blazing eyes, that fierce, passionate, all-consuming kiss...and one night, one dark devil-ridden night, his naked body possessing hers until she drowned in the ecstasy of obsessive passion.

'Was that the phone?' Xenia came padding into the room in a floor-length creamy bathrobe, her long peppery hair streaming wet and loose down her slender back.

'Yes.' Natasha turned to stare, face pale and frightened. 'It was Dominic. He's flying out here tomorrow afternoon.'

Xenia smiled slowly. 'I wondered when he'd turn up. I knew he wouldn't leave it too long...'

Natasha didn't like the way she said that, or the way she looked at her as she spoke. It was as though she knew what was going on, as though she had seen it all coming, long before Natasha herself did, and was simply accepting it as a foregone conclusion.

Well, I won't accept it, Natasha thought frantically.

Hurriedly, she excused herself, went to her bedroom, sitting on the bed and rocking back and forth, trying to control the passions seething under her calm exterior.

Dominic had made no mention of the report on Tony, but she knew he had it, just as surely as he knew that she knew. His cryptic remarks about obsessive love had made it clear to her, and he had enjoyed mocking her, taunting her with his knowledge and his growing understanding of her self, her life, her past.

Did he know she was a virgin? Surely he could only find that out by asking Tony himself, and even then— would one man really tell another that he had had the opportunity to make love to a woman and not taken it? She couldn't believe that. Not one man to another. Didn't most of them try to outdo each other in terms of sexual conquest?

But even that was not the only thing that scared her.

That phone call had been a minefield of terrifying secrets, unveiled at last by Dominic Thorne, the man determined to possess her, and he was so clever, cleverer by far than she had ever realised.

For she herself had only just come to the conclusion that she was very like her great-grandmother, and Dominic had worked it out in nothing more than a split second.

It had taken a lifetime for Natasha to work it out.

She thought suddenly of her mother, smiling at her last week with love and understanding. Her mother had always told her she was like Marie Malakova, that fiery ballerina from a long-forgotten world. Natasha had assumed she meant only in looks. But had her mother really meant that? Or had she seen, from the very beginning, her daughter's capacity for all-consuming passion?

If so, that explained her behaviour when Natasha had fallen for Tony, and made such a fool of herself. Her mother had undoubtedly recognised the cause but felt unable to deal with it, for she herself had always been of stable temperament, calm and loving where Natasha was passionate and wild.

And Dominic knew that too.

He would enjoy, he had said, proving forcibly to her how very much alike they were when he arrived in St Petersburg tomorrow.

That could mean only one thing, and her body rippled with excitement at the thought of it, seeing herself suddenly, naked beneath him as he made wild love to her and reaped the benefits of all that pent-up passion she had been unable to release for a lifetime.

Suddenly, she wanted desperately to release it.

She felt as though she was champing at the bit, ready to tear off her clothes and make frenzied love with him, revel in her freedom, let him plunder her heart, body and soul, let him take all the emotions she had and bathe in them, drown in them, while she drowned in him.

This is so dangerous! she thought fiercely.

I mustn't let it happen.

I must keep control...!

He arrived an hour early, surprising Natasha, who was alone in the living-room waiting for her snack lunch to arrive, when the doorbell of the suite rang, making her jump.

Thinking it might be room service, she went innocently to the door, casually dressed in blue jeans and a white silk camisole top. She nearly fainted with shock to look into that dark, commanding face.

'Dominic...!'

He gave a slow smile. He was dressed impeccably in black, his suit as expensive as it was attractive, the dark red silk tie gleaming against a crisp white shirt, a silver watch-chain across his taut waistcoat.

'Well, hello!' he murmured, studying her from below hooded lids. 'You look even more beautiful than I remembered. I love the silky camisole. Reminds me of the day you burst into my office and tore your clothes off for me...'

'I did no such thing!' she said tightly, stepping away from the door and trying to walk back along the hall into the living-room.

He strode after her, slamming the door, and caught her arm. 'Don't you turn your back on me!'

'Why not?' She looked angrily up at him, trying to get away. 'I'm here to work—not provide entertainment for you!'

'Hours of endless fun, sweetie!' he drawled, eyes mocking. 'And don't spoil it all by telling me you weren't alarmed by our telephone conversation yesterday!'

'I wasn't remotely alarmed.' Her eyes flared angrily. 'I'm stronger than you want to believe—you just haven't got my measure yet!'

'Got all your secrets, though, haven't I?'

Her breath caught with fury. 'What did he say about me? Go on! Tell me! I demand to know what that swine Tony——'

'You can read it for yourself, later tonight, in my bedroom.'

'I don't want to read it!'

'Oh, but you do want to come to my bedroom, don't you?' His gaze dropped to the rise and fall of her breasts, naked beneath the thin silk camisole, nipples extended hard with excitement, heart beating fiercely.

She saw the look of intent darken his eyes, and before he could drag her against his hard body for a kiss, she began to struggle, excited.

At once, he pushed her up against the wall behind her, trapping her there with his body, a hard look on his face.

The brief struggle ended with his victory. She stood silent, breathing hard, staring at the dark red silk tie right in front of her, his chest almost touching her face, and she remembered the way he looked stripped to the waist, his skin tanned, muscles hard, black hairs networking that chest...

She wanted him so much she could barely stand.

'Missed me?'

Terrified, she shook her head.

'Well, I've missed you.' The dark head lowered, and his hot mouth moved slowly, seductively over hers, making a tremor go through her and a slight sigh of pleasure come from her throat.

'Don't...please...' she whispered hoarsely.

'I love it when you say that.'

'But you never stop, do you? You never do what I ask.'

'It's not the words I love,' he drawled thickly, kissing her. 'It's the way you beg...the way you moan... Moan some more for me, darling!' His mouth opened hers and she couldn't help herself, kissing him back with mutual hunger, her arms winding helplessly around his neck, fingers sliding through his dark hair as their tongues and breathing mingled faster...

She was lost rapidly, little moans of need coming from her as she felt his hands move up to her breasts, cupping them through the thin silk camisole, stroking those painful nipples until her mind span dizzily with the words yes, yes, yes...

'Oh, God...!' she whispered hoarsely, almost wanting to grab at his clothes and tear them off. 'Dominic, Dominic...!'

He raised his dark head, breathing thickly, face flushed.

Natasha's lids flickered open, staring with those strange, glittering, obsessive, passionate eyes.

'How deep those rivers run,' Dominic said deeply. 'Fathoms deep, oceans deep... Sometimes I want to drown in your eyes, Natasha, as much as I want to drown in your body.'

'You never will,' she said shakingly. 'I know I can't resist you but I'll have to find a way, because I'll never let you take me to bed, not as long as I live.'

'You won't live very much longer,' he said darkly, 'if you don't.'

'Oh,' she laughed unsteadily, 'you'll kill me, then?'

'Darling, the longer you deny yourself the freedom to make love, the more something deep inside you will die.' He ran one hand over her face, touching the almond-slanting eyelids, the high Slavic cheekbones, the dark, full, bruised red mouth. 'I can't bear to watch this part of you dying, Natasha. This passionate woman, this obsessive lover... and I'll do everything in my power to prevent you from destroying her.'

She stared at him in breathless shock, seeing suddenly that he was right, that he meant what he said, and that his emotions really were engaged with her.

'Why will you, Dominic?' she asked huskily, praying he would say something that would free her, something she needed so desperately to hear before she gave herself to any man, ever. Those three little words that were the only combination which would fit her lock.

'Because I want you,' he drawled thickly, and slid his hand on to her breast again, making her tense with angry excitement even as her heart twisted in bitter pain.

'Still just sex, then?' Her eyes hated him like poison.

'It won't just be sex with us, darling. But I understand why you're scared. Any woman would be, after what you've been through. If I ever meet that arch-swine Tony Kerr, I'll punch his ugly face through the back of his cowardly head.'

She caught her breath, staring into his glittering blue eyes, unable to believe what he'd just said, because it sounded so genuine, and yet how could it be?

'Don't look so surprised, Natasha. You know I have the report.'

'Yes, but I don't understand why you'd see him as the villain of the piece unless——'

'Let's just say you'll be pleasantly surprised by the contents of the report.'

She studied him in breathless silence, afraid to ask what he meant.

'But to find out,' he murmured, kissing her mouth again, 'you'll have to keep that date with destiny, in my bedroom, tonight, when the sun sets on St Petersburg and your past.'

As his mouth opened hers, she found herself unable to deny him this kiss, his words and promises making her lips part with a soft gasp of pleasure, and the kiss was so exciting too, so gorgeous, that she just let it happen, let her eyes close and her head go back and her arms move up around his strong neck.

Passion flared again between them.

Dominic's hands moved up below her camisole to stroke her bare breast again, pressing her firmly against the wall, moving his body against hers slowly, rhythmically, making her moan beneath his mouth with blatant, dizzy desire.

'Did I hear the door——?' Xenia's voice made them both look up, dazed.

They stared at her, their faces flushed, eyes glittering, and Xenia stood shocked for a second, then smiled, and turned without a word to stroll serenely back into the living-room.

'Oops!' Dominic drawled thickly, removing his hand from below her camisole and laughing. 'Oh, well—she was bound to find out sooner or later. At least it means I don't have to tiptoe around trying to seduce you, now.'

'How am I going to work with her?' Natasha said, mortified by what Xenia had seen.

Dominic laughed. 'It's not such a big deal. And what business is it of my mother's, anyway? She employs you. She doesn't own you. As for me—if I hear one word of complaint from her, I'll tell her, politely, to mind her own business. I do what I like in my private life, Natasha, that's what the phrase means. Private. As in, keep out.'

The doorbell rang.

Natasha stared at Dominic and he stared at her.

They had neither of them heard it ring before—they had been too engrossed in their passionate kiss.

'Room service,' Natasha muttered thickly, and went to the door, her face flushed as she realised quite how deeply involved they now were, oblivious to almost everything but each other as they moved deeper and deeper into the dangerous waters of love.

CHAPTER SIX

XENIA said nothing when they joined her in the living-room, moments later, and the waiter wheeled in their snack lunches. In fact she seemed delighted with the situation, a serene smile on her beautiful face as she looked from Dominic to Natasha and back again.

They ate together, the three of them, sitting close to the long windows overlooking the city as the sun shimmered brightly over those fabled gold spires.

'Shall we go out this afternoon?' Dominic suggested at two-thirty. 'I may have joined you here for pleasure——' his gaze shot mockingly at Natasha '—but I don't want to interfere with your work.'

'We wouldn't let you, Dominic.' Xenia laughed. 'Certainly not this afternoon. We have permission to enter the Yusopov palace at three-thirty, and no power on earth would stop me going there.'

'I'm not surprised!' His dark brows shot up. 'My God, even I've never seen it! How did you manage to swing that? Most non-Russians aren't allowed over the threshold.'

'Would you like to come with us?'

'Just try and stop me!' he laughed, with a wicked look at Natasha.

The palace lay on the Moika canal, water glimmering in front of it while the home of the Yusopovs rose in yellow-white crumbling splendour, far more modest on the outside than one would have expected, given the unsurpassed beauty within.

'Rasputin's date with destiny,' Dominic murmured beside Natasha as they walked towards the vast doors.

Her eyes shot darkly to his. 'If that's a reminder of what you want me to do tonight, Dominic, kindly forget it! And especially forget about discussing it while your mother's around.'

'Why? I'm not the one who's ashamed of their own desires—you are.'

'I'm not ashamed of them,' she snapped, and then caught her breath as she saw the beauty of the main staircase, rising in white marble grandeur with lion-sphinxes either side and chandeliers glittering brighter than all the diamonds of Fabergé.

A smart, dark Russian woman with severely disciplined good looks guided them around, jet eyes flickering, long nails unpainted, a black beauty spot above her red lips.

'If all you want,' Natasha murmured in Dominic's ear as he bent his head to listen, 'is a Russian woman—why not take her? She's quite stunning, and clearly very intelligent.'

'She couldn't cope with me, darling,' he drawled wickedly in her ear. 'You're the only one who needs a demon lover—remember?'

She moved away from him, pulses racing, and tried not to think too much about what was building up between them, because she was very much afraid that it would lead into the darkest and most dangerous waters of all—falling violently, obsessively in love.

'Here,' the guide was saying as she guided them from stunning room to stunning room, 'the Yusopovs would give concerts for the imperial family.'

The red-gold concert-hall gleamed under a thousand starry lights.

'And here——' she guided them to a vast dining-room '—they would dine with important guests, rather than in their intimate dining-room...'

Natasha's mind reeled as they went from room to room, along galleries once papered with priceless masterpieces, into ballrooms, dining-rooms, studies, libraries, drawing-rooms, bedrooms...

'In this theatre——' the guide led them down a flight of steps with the Yusopov crest glittering above it '—Anna Pavlova danced in private performance for the Yusopovs and their friends.'

They entered the miniature theatre, red and gold, with a small stage, rows of seats gleaming luxuriously under the lights, while at the back the imperial box glittered pure gold.

'Imagine performances from Anna Pavlova herself...'

'Just think——' Natasha shot him a dark, jealous look '—you could have had your friend Kyra dance specially for you!'

His eyes homed in on her face, narrowing. 'Oh, yes— Kyra. I'd forgotten about her.'

'How cavalier you are!' she said tightly. 'No doubt that'll be how you talk about me in a few years' time. Oh, yes, Natasha—I'd forgotten all about her!'

He laughed. 'No such luck, my darling. I'm afraid I'm a permanent fixture in your life.'

'Oh?' Her heart skidded violently. 'I thought you just wanted to get me into bed?'

'I did and do, believe me, but I'm sure I'll never tire of you.'

'I bet you said that to Kyra, too, five years ago!' She tried to walk away, her face tight and angry.

'You're wrong.' He caught her arm, his voice rough and low. 'I've never said that to any woman. I don't think I've ever felt it.'

She was so afraid to believe that he was telling the truth. It was impossible to trust him. Not when the stakes were so high, and the risk of falling in love so very close, so very near...

'What are you saying?' she asked huskily. 'That there's more to this than just sex?'

'If I said I loved you, what would you say in return?'

'I'd tell you to get lost!'

He studied her in silence for a moment, then bit out thickly, 'Then I'll never say it.'

Her lashes flickered and she looked away, wondering if she had made a mistake, afraid to believe she had, especially after what he had said, because there was no get-out clause for her in his words—any honest emotional response would leave her wide open to look a fool.

They left the theatre and were whisked off again by the guide, taken down to the glittering Arabic room, cool stone, marble and gold-trellised Moorish arches, statues of an Arab man and woman at opposite ends of the temple-like room.

Dominic stood beside Natasha, face hard with anger.

'Are you brooding over something?' Natasha asked huskily.

'Yes,' he said tightly under his breath, bending his head close to her ear. 'I'm brooding over how it will feel to have you in bed tonight.'

Her eyes flared. 'Your mind is a one-track groove!'

'And yours is a convoluted maze poisoned by bitterness and fear.'

She went white, jerking her gaze from his eyes, unable to look him in the face, deeply hurt by his words.

'And now,' said the guide, leading them out of the Arabic room, 'we will see the rooms in which Rasputin was murdered.'

Natasha walked unsteadily beside Dominic, following the others, her face still very pale as those words ran around her mind. Was she really poisoned by bitterness and fear? But she had every right to be afraid of love. Wouldn't anyone be, after what had happened to her?

They went down to the Prince's private rooms, which were decorated with photographs of Rasputin's dead body, documents signed by the Tsar, photographs of the imperial family—the Tsarina, the young haemophiliac Tsarevitch, whose life Rasputin had saved many times.

'Here, the dying Rasputin climbed out of the window,' the guide said, 'and ran across the snowy courtyard, poisoned and bleeding from gunshot wounds...'

Natasha moved close to Dominic. 'What makes you think I'm the only person around here afraid of love? You must be afraid of it, too, or you wouldn't go on about sex all the time.'

He gave a harsh laugh. 'I'm a man. I want your body—not your heart. And I'll get it, tonight, when you come to my room.'

Natasha was about to deliver a blistering reply when the guide said, 'Let us move down to the stone basement where Rasputin was lured, with the promise of a party, to his death.' The irony was not lost on Natasha.

In the stone basement, waxwork figures of Rasputin and Prince Felix were placed at a well-laid table.

'A lamb to the slaughter!' Natasha said tightly, looking at Dominic. 'Much like me, being railroaded into your room tonight!'

'Felix's intentions were good, even if he was a murderer,' Dominic said coldly, eyeing her.

'A pity the same can't be said of your intentions!'

'I'm no murderer.'

'You will be if you make love to me! You know what will happen!'

'Yes,' he said thickly, and his blue eyes blazed with a desire as savage as hers. 'You'll finally unleash yourself on me, I'll possess you utterly—and it's what I want more than anything else in the world!'

She gasped in despair and backed away from him, eyes glittering strangely, then turned and ran up the stairs, running blindly along golden corridors for ages until she was outside, panting for breath, leaning against the creamy yellow walls as the sun danced on the canal.

Xenia and Dominic appeared minutes later, just as Natasha got her breath back. The car slid up towards them as soon as the chauffeur saw them emerge.

'Ah,' drawled Dominic with a hard smile, 'the sulking Natasha. I'm rather afraid, Mama, that I upset her dreadfully just now. Perhaps I should take her to dinner alone tonight to make up for it?'

'I'd rather die——' began Natasha in a furious voice.

'What a good idea!' Xenia said at exactly the same moment. 'I'm so tired, I could do with a night on my own, and it will be nice for you to have a dinner à deux!'

'That's settled, then,' drawled Dominic, his eyes glittering with demonic intent as he smiled mockingly at Natasha.

Rigid with fury, aware that he had trapped her again, Natasha rode back in the limousine in tense silence, avoiding his eyes and staring angrily at the streets of St Petersburg.

Back at the hotel, she took a long scented bath, struggling to understand his passionate words. He said he wanted her to unleash herself on him—and clearly he knew that that unleashing would be more than sexual.

Yet he still wanted it. All of it. Did that mean he loved her?

God, she was so scared of lying to herself, letting her imagination run riot as it leapt from unreal clue to unreal clue. If he really loved her, he wouldn't keep going on about sex all the time, would he?

And yet...she couldn't help knowing that the moment Dominic really turned hostile and emotional was the moment they spoke of love, in that beautiful little theatre where Pavlova had danced.

She had said she would tell him to get lost if he told her he loved her. 'Then I'll never say it,' he had replied, and Natasha's heart melted with desperate hope, for she wanted so much to believe that he did love her. She wanted it more than anything else.

That was what made it so dangerous.

Obsessive love was clamouring to get out, champing at the bit, yearning to direct its scorching rays on Dominic Thorne, and she knew it would not take much more pressure from him to make her keel over and fall, just drop like a body from a tall building, screaming in anticipation of total destruction...unless he held out the safety-net of love.

He's got to love me, she thought, tears burning her eyes.

He's got to love me or I can't give myself to him, I can't let myself give in to this overwhelming desire, not like this, not when he's made it so clear that he doesn't care, won't give up anything in return for——

Suddenly, she remembered Kyra.

All jealousy aside, Dominic had once promised her that he would tell her about Kyra if she told him about

Tony. But he knew about Tony now, didn't he? And although she hadn't told him, it was hardly a fair exchange.

She got out of the bath, excited at the memory of that promise. At least it gave her *something* to bargain with.

He came to the suite to get her at eight. She was ready for him, dressed in a gold silk shift dress, a veil of dark brown chiffon softly draped over it, giving seductive mystery to her slender curves.

'Superb...' he murmured softly, eyes burning like blue fire over her body. 'I can't wait to slowly remove it!'

'You'll wait for eternity!' she said fiercely, lifting her head.

He laughed under his breath. 'We'll see...' and took her wrist in his possessive hand, leading her along the corridor to the lifts.

Downstairs, green malachite pillars gleamed in more than imperial splendour, chandeliers glistened softly overhead, statues stood in alcoves close to expensive, mirrored bars, and Cartier's welcomed customers in a black-carpeted, luxurious, dim-lit showroom.

As they entered the restaurant at the end of the corridor, the head waiter swept up to them and bowed low. 'Welcome back, Mr Thorne,' he said in Russian. 'A table for two? Follow me...'

They were given a very quiet table in a corner of the restaurant. Dominic ordered a bottle of champagne to be brought on ice, and then they both chose fresh caviare served with tiny blini pancakes and chilled vodka. Natasha chose grilled sole while Dominic preferred beef stroganoff.

'Don't sit there fulminating,' Dominic drawled as they ate their caviare. 'People might think you hate me.'

'I do hate you! But then, you hate me too, so we're even!'

'Not just yet, we're not,' he drawled, and his blue eyes glittered in the flickering candle-flame, light and shadow playing on his hard-boned face, emphasising the dramatic contours of his tough features.

Her heart skipped obsessive beats of love. She moistened her lips, the salt-fresh tang of caviare delicious, and tried not to think of how deeply she wanted him, because she knew how much danger she was in.

Don't delay too long, she thought. You have to make sure he talks about Kyra before you go upstairs with him—if you go upstairs at all.

'You once made a deal with me,' she said tightly. 'You said that you would tell me about Kyra if I told you about Tony.'

His eyes narrowed. 'Oh, yes... I'd forgotten about that.'

'Well, you already know everything about me and Tony—don't you? So why should I bother to come upstairs? I don't need to know what that report says—I already know the whole story backwards!'

The waiter appeared suddenly, clearing their plates away while Dominic watched Natasha with narrowed eyes.

'I told you,' he said when they were alone again. 'There's something you don't expect in that report. You must read it.'

'Tell me what it is now, and I'll consider going to your bedroom.'

He rapped long fingers on the table. 'No deal.'

'OK, then!' She faced him, eyes glittering. 'No deal.'

The waiter appeared again, delivering their main course.

When they were alone again with food neither wanted to eat, Dominic said, 'This is your price, is it? I give you a brief run-down on Kyra, and you come to my bedroom after dinner?'

'That's my price.'

He rapped his long fingers on the table again, eyes narrowed, then came to a quick decision. 'All right, then. I'll tell you about Kyra.'

Natasha sat back, eyes dark, listening.

'I fell in love with her five years ago,' he said flatly. 'And I pursued her relentlessly. I thought at first she was playing hard to get, and then I realised she wasn't, but by then it was too late—I was obsessively in love.'

Natasha's eyes flashed to his face. Her heart stopped beating, then gave a sickening lurch, thundering back into life as she thought of what he had said on the phone yesterday, how he would enjoy proving forcibly to her that he could cope with obsessive, passionate love.

'I couldn't stop wanting her,' he said coolly, 'but she was seeing someone else. He was a real wimp—I couldn't understand what the hell she saw in him. Especially with me around, arrogant as I was, because she was so beautiful, talented and lively—and I'm so dynamic. How could she possibly prefer that tongue-tied little mummy's boy to a man like me?'

'How indeed . . .?' murmured Natasha, smiling, her eyes intense.

'It was a terrible blow to my ego,' said Dominic, 'but I was in too deep by then. I was obsessed with Kyra, and so I refused to take notice of her preference for the wimp. I chased her and chased her and . . .'

'For how long?'

'Just over a year. It was the most all-consuming obsession I'd ever felt. I did everything you're not supposed to do. Hung around the stage door waiting for her, sent her endless bouquets, rang her up in the early hours of the morning, turned up on her doorstep...'

Natasha stared fascinated, her heart beating an obsessive rhythm of love, desire, passionate empathy. She felt as though his words were touching her soul, bonding with it in joint understanding.

'Then one night I lost control,' he said softly, 'and tried to kiss her. She slapped my face and told me to get lost. She loathed men like me. Found me and my fiery passion repellent. She preferred her little mummy's boy, with his spindly body and old-fashioned clothes and sweet, stupid, totally sexless smile.'

'How awful for you...'

'Worse than that. It totally destroyed my confidence for a year. I couldn't bring myself to look at another woman, let alone ask her out.'

Natasha was breathless. 'She damaged you...'

'Badly,' he agreed with a sardonic smile. 'And I got caught up in a vicious circle of shattered ego and lost confidence. In the end, I got so angry with the whole thing that I decided to find out every last detail about her, just so I could understand what had happened a little better. I set my team of detectives on her trail, and guess what I discovered?'

Natasha shook her head rigidly.

'She had been brutally raped three weeks before I met her.'

'Oh, my God...!' Natasha said in horror. 'No wonder she preferred the wimp! You must have terrified the life out of her. Just one look at you would tell any woman that you were a passionate, red-blooded swine!'

'How very revealing of you to say so,' he drawled softly, eyes glittering, and her heart whacked with fierce desire against her chest.

'You know what I meant!'

'Ah, but do you know what I meant by telling you about Kyra's past, and how it had directly affected me?'

She hesitated, afraid to answer directly.

'It freed me from her spell, Natasha, just as reading that report I have upstairs will free you.' His face was tough, his ego powerful, and his sense of himself as a man formidable. 'Because, you see, while Tony Kerr wasn't raped, he was already badly damaged when you met him—a fact you will discover when you come to my bedroom in——' he glanced at the Cartier watch on his hair-roughened wrist '—shall we say five minutes?'

Natasha hesitated, heart beating fast. 'So soon?'

'That's the deal, Natasha!' he bit out thickly, and signalled for the bill.

They went upstairs minutes later.

As soon as Dominic let her into his suite, his mood changed, eyes darkening with desire as he took her by the wrist and led her into his bedroom.

She stood there, trembling inside.

The black file lay in the centre of the dark-canopied bed. Gold light glowed across the deep-carpeted floor. Long lace curtains flickered in the warm breeze from the fractionally open windows. Outside, the night was black indeed, black as that file.

'Read it,' he murmured beside her.

She obeyed, walking to the bed, sinking down on to it and picking up the file, flipping it open, beginning to read.

At once, her eyes widened in shock.

Dominic closed the door, shrugged out of his jacket and began lazily unbuttoning his dark waistcoat, loosening his tie, then strolling coolly to the bedside table to pour two glasses of brandy.

Natasha prickled with intense sexual awareness, her eyes shot to admire his powerful body, and then he shot her a look, his smile mockingly aware that she wanted him more than she wanted to read about Tony.

Had it really come to that? Natasha thought in astonishment, staring at his hard, commanding face.

Here she had a detailed report on Tony, telling her precisely why he had damaged her so badly—and all she could think of was Dominic's kiss, his body, that black waistcoat temptingly unbuttoned, his tie loosened, and his stance as he poured the brandy enough to make her weak with desire.

Quickly, she bent her head and read on, eyes darting down the page, struggling to ignore Dominic.

'Here.' He handed her a glass of brandy.

She took it without looking at him, but she felt the brush of his long fingers and shivered, then continued to read, forcing herself to concentrate.

Dominic sank on to the bed beside her, kicked off his shoes, stretched out lazily, his dark head against the pillows as he watched her from below those heavy eyelids.

She pretended not to be aware of him, but he smiled as he saw the hot, brooding look she gave him, and he knew what she wanted, but he was not prepared to give it to her until she had read that report.

She forced herself to read on.

Time ticked away. Outside, the dim sound of traffic in the St Petersburg streets was a steady hum in the quiet bedroom.

'I can't believe it!' Natasha said thickly as she finished the report. 'It's like reading about a totally different man—a stranger.'

'Clearly incapable of any kind of relationship.'

'Yes.' She stared at him. 'And I blamed myself for it all!'

'That's what he wanted you to do. That's why he lied to you.' He smiled sardonically. 'I was particularly interested in his forty-eight-hour marriage. I'm sure he never told you about that, did he? No, I didn't think he would have done. Far too revealing.'

'It's very clear from this report that he only married her out of desperation to stop people talking,' she agreed.

'Well, he was pushing forty, he'd lived in the same village all his life, sharing that cottage with his mother——'

'Who spent half her life in and out of mental institutions.' She was still reeling in amazement from that one. 'Another thing he never told me.'

'And he'd never been involved with a woman,' drawled Dominic. 'No wonder he married out of desperation, and hardly surprisingly the marriage only lasted forty-eight hours.'

Natasha shook her head, staring down at the file open on her gold-brown silk and chiffon lap. 'He'd never had any relationship at all. Not real ones, not man-woman...'

'But he was too frightened to face what that said about him.' Dominic sipped his brandy contemplatively. 'So, as soon as his mother died, he packed up, moved to Ashford, and set out to live a lie.'

'I met him the month he arrived in town,' Natasha said thickly. 'I believed his sad story about having just been deserted by his live-in girlfriend of fifteen years.'

'No doubt he described this fictitious woman in great detail?'

'Down to the last red ringlet of her hair.'

There was a brief silence. Dominic watched her from the pillows, his body sprawled with masculine grace, one long leg bent, one arm resting on it, cradling the brandy glass in long fingers while his blue eyes gleamed dark and possessive on her face.

'He kept telling me,' Natasha remembered, fighting her desire for Dominic with everything she had, 'that he didn't believe my love was sincere. He needed proof, and lots of it, but he couldn't bring himself to demand so much of me because I was so young, that's why he was leaving me. I thought he wanted me to chase after him.'

'And you did,' he said softly, 'like a lamb to the slaughter.'

She gave him a dark, angry look. 'It wasn't my fault! He conned me into it!'

'Oh, I agree. But never forget that he couldn't have conned you if you hadn't been capable of such extremes of emotion.' His eyes darkened. 'Such obsessive love.'

She thought of him with Kyra, of his capacity for obsessive desire, and the way it had damaged his life, too. He had solved it by getting a detailed report on Kyra. And now he had done the same for her, determined to break the hold of that vicious circle on her.

She felt sudden waves of burning emotion, both for him as a man and for him as the man who had got her this report, for she saw now that it had changed her life.

He had changed her life—Dominic Thorne.

Afraid of the emotions building up inside her, she looked away from him, letting the file slide off her lap, putting it back on the bed and staring at it, her heart thudding fast as she struggled to find the words she needed to thank him with.

'I...' Her voice was husky. 'I don't know how to thank you for getting that report for me. It—it really does change everything.'

He watched her in silence, a smile playing on his hard mouth.

'I haven't had time,' she went on, 'to fully assimilate all the information, but it undoubtedly will change my life, and I'm very grateful to you for getting it.'

'Care to thank me properly?' he said softly.

Her heart nose-dived into sickening excitement, and she looked hotly at him through her lashes across the dimly lit bed.

'What exactly do you mean?' she whispered, though she knew.

'Well, now,' he murmured, 'that report on Tony Kerr makes me fairly certain that he was a virgin, regardless of his brief marriage.'

Natasha stared with dark eyes as her face and body burned.

'And if he was a virgin,' Dominic said softly, 'what does that make you?'

'Don't...' she whispered huskily, looking away.

'I understand that you're scared.' His voice was so seductive she almost bathed in the caress of its dark tones. 'So I'm not going to leap on you. But I do want you, Natasha, and I know—I just know you want to thank me properly for what I've done for you.'

Her breathing accelerated as she raised hot, dark eyes to his.

'So why don't I just leave it all up to you?' he said smokily, watching her through those heavy, lowered eyelids from the pillow. 'I'm sure you know how much I'd appreciate a kiss and a whispered thank you...'

Her breath sucked in slowly with excitement, and she found it irresistible, her eyes moving over his body as he lay there, watching her, knowing how much she wanted to do exquisite things...

Suddenly, she felt brave because he had given her the choice, and before she knew it, she was moving towards him like a passion-hungry lioness on her hands and knees, green eyes glittering intently.

Sliding her body against his, her heart banged violently as she lowered her red head to kiss his strong throat.

He gave a rough groan of pleasure, one hand moving up to stroke her hair, running his fingers through it as her mouth sucked passionately at his throat.

Breathing rapidly, she slid one thigh over his strong legs, and rocked her body against him, let her head move up, her mouth meeting his in passionate kisses that he enjoyed without moving a muscle.

'Thank you,' she whispered, and ran her hands over his chest, growing bolder, sliding his waistcoat apart, beginning to unbutton his shirt.

He exhaled hotly, closing his eyes.

Her hands slid each button apart as her mouth drank from his, tongues and breathing mingling hotly, her body rocking seductively against his hard thigh as her fingers worked slowly, slowly, until his shirt was open and she was able to push it off, along with his waistcoat, leaving him bare-chested, his heart thudding hard.

'Thank you...' she whispered again, and she loved the feel of his chest beneath her hungry fingertips, the rough black hairs, the hot flesh, the powerful muscles.

Sexual excitement was rising in her as she kissed him deeply, stroking his chest, letting him lie back with eyes closed. He loved every second of her slavish worship of his body, and she loved it too, excited by her master, and by her own slavery.

He groaned as she ran her hands boldly over his hips, then his hard thighs, making him move against her, pressing up, the rigid manhood burning beneath the dark material of his trousers—burning for her touch.

Shaking with excitement, she let her hand slide softly over its pulsating hardness.

His breath expelled in a hot gasp of stunned pleasure, and he said thickly, 'Yes . . . yes!'

'Thank you . . .' she whispered, stroking it slowly, provocatively, and he groaned hoarsely, his mouth passionate beneath her as he lay on his back, stripped to the waist, his eyes closed, whispering her name incoherently as she continued to stroke him.

Natasha kissed him deeply, unbearably aroused, not only by her unexpected success as a seductress, but also burning with desire, touching the most powerful symbol of masculinity, feeling it pulse and jerk. She had always wondered how it would feel to touch, had known deep inside that with the right man it would feel like this— so good, so good . . .

His hands moved up her spine to the zip of her dress, and she felt him slide it down over her shoulders, down to her waist. She shuddered as his hands unhooked her bra, letting it fall to the floor.

'Thank you . . .' she said again, bare-breasted, eyes tightly closed, gently rocking herself against his hard thigh, and his hands moved over her, fingers sliding swiftly to touch her, cupping her aching breasts, stroking the painfully erect nipples.

The kiss grew more passionate still as they began to lose themselves in the dark currents of sexual excitement.

'Oh, thank you...' Natasha moaned blindly against his mouth, and his long, hoarse groan as he heard her say it again made the burning wetness between her thighs burn more. She rocked herself gently against his hard thigh, lost in dark desire, her hand stroking him, feeling his hard flesh jerk and throb beneath her fingers.

'Oh, God!' he bit out thickly, driven beyond control.

Suddenly, she was flung on to her back, he was pressing down on her, his eyes burning hot, his face darkly flushed, and as his hard mouth closed fiercely over hers, he reached up to punch out the light.

Darkness fell on them, and Natasha moaned underneath the hot onslaught of his kiss.

Lying on her back, her thighs parted for him as he touched her bare breasts, she wanted him so much she could almost taste him, almost feel his naked flesh merging with hers, and the aching wetness between her thighs cried out for satisfaction.

He was just as urgent, one hand pulling her dress down over her hips, dropping it to the floor, leaving her naked but for lace panties, damp with excitement.

'Dominic...!' she said shakily against his mouth and let her thighs slip apart for his long-fingered hands to stroke, instinctively letting go of the last shreds of fear in her tormented desire for him.

'Oh, darling!' His mouth was passionate and insistent, his hand between her spread thighs, a fierce groan coming from his throat as he touched the hot, damp silk and heard her cry out in appalled desire. 'I won't hurt you, I promise, I'll make love to you like——'

'No...' Her voice was muffled against his mouth as she tried to slow this down, slow him down, get it back to a manageable stage of arousal.

'Darling!' He slipped his hand beneath the thin silk, breathing hoarsely as he touched the softly curling hair, then groaning long and loud as his finger encountered the hot, slippery-wet flesh.

Natasha's body screamed for satisfaction. She cried out with guttural pleasure as his finger slipped inside her, making her want to go on, go all the way, strip him naked too, and welcome that rigid, pulsating hardness into her body.

'Oh, God!' Her breath was coming faster, she was moving against his hand, her legs softly spread and her body throbbing with heat. 'I didn't mean it to go this far...I want to stop...' but her body told a different story. She moved faster against his hand, moaning hoarsely, and then his hands stroked her panties down over her hips, her slender thighs.

'Darling...' He had her naked, his heart was banging like a demented hammer, his hands trembling as they ran over her body.

'No...' She tried to fight him, pushing at his broad shoulders.

'Darling...darling...' he groaned raggedly, and his finger slid into her hot slippery flesh again, making her moan against his mouth, excited and afraid as her legs splayed in helpless, slavish excitement.

'No...'

His mouth silenced her protests as his finger stroked her hot flesh to serious arousal, and as she began to gasp and shudder, her fear rose parallel with her excitement, but she could not stop wanting it, this exquisite freedom, the gnawing of sexual desire in her body, the desperation to release it all on him.

She felt the fierce, violent, intensely necessary orgasm building. She felt possessed by a demonic excitement. Her heart was galloping, blood pounding round her body. She shouted, cried out, moving her naked body against his hand with wanton desire for the ecstasy she had never allowed herself before—and which only he could give her.

Dominic groaned out loud, took his hand away from her just before she was able to orgasm, and as she writhed, naked and desperate for satisfaction, he began to undo his black trousers.

She saw him through a mist of blazing fear and excitement. If he took her, she would be lost, finished, smashed to death on the rocks of obsessive passion.

'No...don't...' Scared, dizzy, she pushed at his chest.

'Natasha...!' He fumbled with the zip of his trousers, and as she heard it flare down, common sense hit her like a bullet.

'No!' she screamed, and this time she really meant it. She took him off guard with a blow to the stomach which knocked him sideways long enough for her to scramble off the bed, shaking like an animal.

Snatching up her dress, she pulled it on while Dominic rolled over, leapt off the bed, zipping his trousers up and striding over to her with a face like dark thunder, eyes glittering fiercely.

'What the hell do you think you're doing?' he demanded hoarsely.

'Leaving!' Her voice shook as she tugged the dress up over her shoulders.

'At this point!' He towered over her in black-eyed rage and his voice shook with excitement and emotion. 'Are you out of your mind?'

'I must have been!' She fumbled, shaking too as she reached behind her for the zip of her dress. 'To let it get this far!'

'Do you seriously think I'm going to let you just walk out? After that? And leave me in this condition?'

'I'm sure you can take care of it!'

'You little——'

'Why not? I've been living like that all my life—why shouldn't you try it for the night?'

'Because I've got a hot and passionate woman,' he said thickly, staring down at her in the darkness with fierce blue eyes, 'who needs to make love to me as badly as I need to make love to her.'

'That's . . .' Her eyes closed in savage pain. 'That's not a good enough reason.'

'Then what is?' he said, his voice jagged and his eyes black. 'Tell me the answer you need to hear and I'll see if I can give it.'

'I need love, Dominic,' she said fiercely. 'This kind of relationship is beyond me. I can't cope with it—don't you understand that?' Her eyes searched his. 'You know me now! You know what will happen to me if I let myself act on this sexual attraction between us! I'll end up either damaged beyond repair or falling wildly in love with you!' She swallowed, her heart banging hard. 'Is—is that really what you want, Dominic? To make me fall wildly in love with you? To inflict more damage on me than I know how to handle?'

'I don't want to damage you,' he said roughly, staring deep into her eyes. 'But why should I love you when you so clearly don't love me?'

Helplessly trapped by that question, she shook her head.

He drew a harsh breath, studied the top of her head with angry eyes and drawled tightly, 'So, are you going to stay or not?'

Natasha flinched at the contemptuous tone of his voice and wrenched herself away from him. 'Never in a million years!'

Turning, she snatched up her shoes and ran out of the room before the tears came, streaming down her cheeks in hot, wet misery.

He didn't bother to follow her.

She let herself into her own suite, stumbled, blind with tears, to the bedroom, and sank down weeping on the bed. If he didn't stop pursuing her soon, she was going to fall so deeply in love with him that he would make the damage Tony inflicted on her look like nothing.

The trouble was—she was beginning to think it might be too late.

CHAPTER SEVEN

IT WAS a long night for her, plagued by dreams. First, she dreamt that she was at her family's home in Kent, and that the doorbell rang. She saw the doorbell clearly in her mind—a dark wood hexagon with a white button in the centre of it. Dominic's was the finger pressing it, making it ring, and her last thought before waking was, I'll never be lonely again.

Jacknifing up in bed, covered in sweat, Natasha stared into the darkness of her hotel bedroom.

He hardly wanted to rescue her from loneliness. Not when all he wanted was sex. And besides—she had never thought of herself as lonely. Not really.

Denying herself grand passion was hardly akin to extreme loneliness. She had lots of friends, a busy life, plenty to do. How could she possibly be lonely?

Or had she always been lonely, she wondered, staring into the darkness. Was that what the dream was telling her? That she had been lonely all her life, without ever knowing it, and that meeting Dominic with his similar—obsessive, passionate, wildly emotional—personality, was going to heal that unnoticed loneliness forever.

Gradually her breathing returned to normal, and she found herself drifting slowly into sleep.

She dreamt that Dominic sat at a piano, composing a classical symphony. 'It's for you,' he said, and when she looked closely at the piano, she saw it was decorated with a gold crest—the double-headed eagle of imperial Russia.

Again, she woke up covered in sweat, darkness all around her, and again she found herself trying to understand the dream.

Had there been more to her unknown loneliness than she yet realised? Was Dominic's Russian ancestry an important link between them? And did he love her already? Was he harbouring the same secret, obsessive emotion for her that she was harbouring for him? Was that what her dreams were telling her? They were hardly dreams of menace or danger—quite the reverse. They were images of true love.

But love *is* dangerous, she thought, curling up beneath the duvet, her eyes frightened.

Love is dangerous...

In the morning, she awoke to find sunlight flooding in over the luxurious bedroom, and the sound of the television playing in the living-room next door.

Getting up, she padded into the lounge.

'Morning...' She smiled sleepily at Xenia, who was eating breakfast at a silver trolley, watching the international news programme.

'Oh, good morning, dear!' Xenia gave her a big smile. 'Did you have a lovely time last night? I heard you come in very late...'

Natasha flushed scarlet and walked to the window to look out, trying to cover her embarrassment. 'Yes, I had a lovely time.' Her eyes scanned the busy street below. 'Another beautiful day today! Haven't we been lucky with the weather?'

'St Petersburg only has around thirty days of sunshine each year. We've had three of them.' Xenia drank her coffee. 'We'll be going to Tsarskoe Selo today. Let's hope the weather keeps up.'

Natasha turned, pulses leaping. 'Is Dominic coming with us?'

'Of course. He's on his way here now.'

The doorbell rang as the words left her lips, and Natasha nearly jumped out of her skin, haunted green eyes flashing to the hallway.

'Let him in, would you, dear?' Xenia murmured softly.

Natasha hesitated, aware of her sleepy appearance, the blue silk nightdress revealing a glimpse of white breasts, the straps tiny on her slim shoulders, her hair tousled around her dramatically beautiful face.

The doorbell rang again.

Xenia looked at her with a serene smile and said again, softly, 'Do let him in, darling.'

With a jerky nod, Natasha went to the hallway, dithering, wondering if she should get her dressing-gown before answering the door, but before she could slip into her bedroom, the doorbell rang again, and she didn't dare cause a scene by letting him stay out there much longer.

As soon as she opened the door, she saw his angry blue eyes and hard mouth, and her heart gave a sickening lurch. She had to avoid his eyes for fear of revealing her by now overwhelming feelings.

'Good morning,' he said bitingly, as though he would rather stick a knife in her than be polite.

At once, she turned her back on him, folding her arms across her scantily clad body, face burning with the memory of last night, and how she had spread out nude for him, moaning with excitement.

'There's a welcoming sight!' Dominic was enraged by her behaviour, stepping into the hall and closing the door with an angry slam behind him. 'Do you turn your back on every man you strip naked for? Or——'

'Don't you dare try to shame me!' she whispered fiercely, turning to stare at him with blazing green eyes. 'Making it sound like a private strip-tease for your benefit!'

'Tease being the appropriate word.'

'No! Mistake, Dominic! What happened between us last night was a mistake. Worse than that, it was dangerous. So dangerous that I should be commended for stopping it!'

He strode towards her, face angry. 'That's medal-winning talk, Natasha. We're lovers, not people being awarded for bravery on the battlefield.' He lowered over her, blue eyes blazing as they scanned her face with a potent mixture of hatred and desire. 'Although sometimes with you it seems very like a battlefield!'

'Yes...it does, doesn't it?'

'At least we agree on something,' he said thickly, angrily. 'And you've fought me every step of the way so far. Maybe I shouldn't be surprised that you're still fighting.'

'I always will, Dominic.'

'You didn't last night.' A smile touched the hard mouth and his hands began slowly to caress her bare shoulders, making her shiver. 'On the contrary, you proved a remarkable temptress...'

'I was tired and emotional.' She bent her head, flushing.

'No, you were genuine,' he said softly. 'You meant every second of it, especially at the beginning, when you thanked me so exquisitely, with your hands and your kisses...'

Natasha drew in her breath, excited at the memory, and her eyes flashed up with hot, secret emotion to meet his.

Their gazes locked with mutual desire.

'Didn't think much more about Tony, did you?' he said thickly. 'I found your indifference to him as exciting as your hunger for me.'

'You wanted to knock him out of my head from the beginning!'

'Have I succeeded?'

'You know you have.'

'What about your heart, Natasha?' His dark eyes searched hers. 'Is there any trace of him left there?'

'Not even a whisper.'

Dominic bent his dark head, kissing her mouth, fiercely, possessively, and she responded at once, helpless to resist him, her head going back, her eyes closing, and her mouth opening hotly beneath his.

'You're mine, then?' he said against her mouth.

'Never!' she whispered, but her arms were strong around his neck, her body was pressing against his, and the passion in her kiss more than betrayed her true feelings.

Her response inflamed him, and soon his hands were moving over her body, excited by her nudity beneath the thin silk nightdress, long fingers sliding down the strap on her left shoulder, his hot mouth kissing her skin as he tugged the bodice down to bare her breast, and as his hand caressed it, stroked the erect nipple, Natasha gave a hoarse moan of longing.

'Oh, God...!' Dominic said thickly, and then his head swooped, hot mouth sucking at her nipple while she flung back her head, moaning with pleasure, running her fingers through his hair.

Hot needles of overwhelming desire were shooting through her. She wanted him to make love to her, right now, just take her into the bedroom and give her what she so badly needed.

The reality of her emotions frightened her.

'Don't...!' she whispered, dizzily pulling away, her heart banging so hard that she thought she would faint. 'We mustn't do this any more...it's so dangerous, Dominic, so very dangerous!'

'Why is it?' he demanded, raising his head, refusing to release her, his face darkly flushed. 'It's what we both want.'

She looked dazedly into his eyes and murmured, 'Yes...it is...but we mustn't have it.'

'Why? Because you're afraid?'

'I told you last night!' Her eyes blazed passionately. 'I won't go to bed with you! Not like this, not without love, not without some kind of emotional involvement that's going to last longer than the time it takes to get my clothes off!'

'I had them all off last night! I'm still here, still interested, still unable to keep my hands off you. What more do you want?'

Angrily, she pushed at his broad shoulders. 'Love! Nothing more and nothing less!'

His body tensed, a muscle jerking in his cheek as he looked down at her with hating eyes and said bitingly, 'I gave you my answer to that last night.'

'Then we should understand each other.' She felt stabbed, looking away, trying to keep her feelings under control.

'Yes.' His voice thickened. 'We should understand each other. Ours is purely a physical attraction. So let's hear no more refusals from you, my darling. Tonight——'

'I am not coming to your room again tonight!'

'Oh, yes, you are, or I won't take you to the ballet.'
Natasha stared for a second. 'The ballet...?'

'*Swan Lake,*' he said softly, 'at the Kirov.'

Everything she had ever loved about her great-grand-mother and Russia came whirling into her mind as she felt, in her heart, the music-box open, saw the tiny ballerina spinning slowly in arabesque, reflected in that gold-framed mirror while the tinny gold music sphere played *Swan Lake*.

Oh...how could she refuse? Her great green eyes stared wildly into his, all the tragedy and romance of her ancestor reflected in herself.

'I have the only tickets left in St Petersburg.' Dominic clinched his victory with a mocking smile. 'And the price, my love, is once again a night in my room.'

Angrily, she pushed away from him. 'I'd rather die!'

'One hour, then,' he drawled, holding on to her and laughing.

'No!'

'Forty-five minutes?'

She studied him with obsessive slanting eyes, thinking of the Kirov, of *Swan Lake*, of that music-box.

'Thirty minutes,' Dominic said softly. 'And that's my final offer.'

'Five minutes,' she heard her voice say.

He smiled slowly, then drawled, 'Twenty-five.'

'Ten!'

'Twenty!'

'Fifteen!'

'Done!' He laughed under his breath, that excited glitter returning to his blue eyes. 'Let's seal the bargain with a kiss!'

Before she could move, he had swept her into his arms again, kissing her long and deep, hands moving over her body until one cupped her rear excitingly, the other cradling her head, fingers tunnelling into dark, soft red hair, his eyes tightly closed and his mouth passionate.

Natasha's arms wound around his neck, her mouth open hungrily beneath his, soft moans of desire wrung from her, as they always were, whenever he touched or kissed her.

Dominic raised his dark head from her, breathing thickly. 'Oh, God, with a woman like you, a lot can happen in fifteen minutes!'

She blushed angrily, breathless with desire for him. 'I shall have to see that nothing happens! Nothing at all!'

'You and me alone on a bed?' he drawled.

'I can hold you off!'

'Well, if you care to take a bet on it...?'

'No, I don't.' Natasha pulled away from him, still dizzy from his kiss, and shot him a hot look under her lashes. 'What I care to do right now is get dressed. If you'll excuse me...' She walked away to her bedroom, head held high, and closed the door on his soft, mocking laughter.

She was smiling, though, even as she went to the bathroom to shower, because no matter what else she could say about Dominic, he did keep doing wonderful things for her.

Swan Lake at the Kirov...!

It would be worth going to his room again for that, and the truth was that she did want to go to his room, she knew she did, deep in her secret, obsessive heart; she wanted to make love with him.

Turning under the warm needles of water, she closed her eyes, soaped her body, remembering his touch last night, and shuddering at the memory of that intense orgasm, approaching fast, so quickly lost, making her cry out and clutch his naked back ... If only he had said he loved her, if only they could make love *with* love, she would be able to release herself, let herself go completely, not hold back as she did last night.

Natasha enjoyed the fantasy, leaning against the wall, her hands touching her own body and imagining they were his.

Then she thought: but he doesn't love me!

Her eyes opened with terrible pain. She stared across the shimmering jets of water, and saw herself in the mirror, a naked woman alone with her dreams, her fantasies, and no love.

It hurt her so deeply that she began to cry, and she wondered as she wept into the water how many more tears Dominic would make her cry before she found the strength to end this damaging relationship with him.

Ten minutes later, she got out of the shower, blow-dried her long red hair, and began to get dressed, choosing a bright yellow sundress to try and cheer herself up, teaming it with flat, gold sandals.

Dominic smiled when she entered the living-room. 'You look good enough to eat!'

She gave him a hot, angry, hating look and ignored him.

'Cross about something?' he drawled, eyes narrowing as he strode over to her, bent to kiss her mouth.

Natasha jerked her face away, and his kiss landed on her cheek.

He raised his dark head, anger in his eyes as he drawled tightly, 'Look at this, Mama! She's angry with me for asking her to the Kirov tonight! Who would have thought——?'

'When are we leaving for Tsarskoe Selo?' Natasha cut in deliberately, refusing to rise to his bait, angry that he was using something so precious to her—*Swan Lake* at the Kirov—to blackmail her back into bed, without love or respect or good intentions. 'Shouldn't we go soon?'

'We were waiting for you, dear.' Xenia put her handbag over her arm. 'The car's been downstairs for twenty minutes.'

Mortified, Natasha grabbed her own handbag from the chair, and as they all left the suite Dominic was keeping his temper with difficulty, giving her hard, angry looks that told her he wanted to shake her till her teeth rattled for the way she had just treated him.

Natasha ignored him. What did he expect, she thought angrily, when he had set out deliberately from the beginning to get her into bed and would clearly stop at nothing? He had been banking on her inability to resist his kisses, and of course, she still couldn't resist them, no matter how she tried.

I want him, she thought, her eyes hot and obsessive as she stared at him through her lashes. I want him and I might not be able to resist him again tonight.

But that doesn't mean I have to be polite to him. Certainly not if he doesn't even care about my feelings, let alone feel any love for me.

The limousine glinted in the sunlight outside. They got into the luxurious rear, all three of them together, and Dominic sat opposite Natasha, his face hard with fury.

He wanted to know why she was ignoring him, of course, but she didn't see why she should even look at him, let alone tell him what was bothering her.

Xenia had to talk most of the time to keep the atmosphere from becoming tense.

'Of course,' Xenia was saying as they drove along, 'Tsarskoe Selo was renamed Pushkin after the revolution.'

'But it originally meant "the Tsar's Village",' Natasha said with a smile, avoiding Dominic's eyes and talking only to Xenia. 'Catherine the Great had it built as a sort of fairy-tale retreat, acres of parkland, palaces, lakes and gardens, all strictly for the imperial family's use.'

'The last Tsar spent all his time there,' Xenia agreed. 'He was very much a countryman at heart. He hated matters of state and the artifice of court life. That's why he lost his empire, poor boy.'

'He was arrested and imprisoned at Tsarskoe Selo, wasn't he? I——'

'Must we talk incessantly about Russian history?' Dominic cut in harshly, deliberately finding a way to end the conversation which Natasha was using to exclude him. 'I'm not in the mood for it.'

'It's my job,' Natasha said tightly. 'And I—'

'Well, you can wait till we get there to talk about it. In the meantime—shut up.'

Natasha fell silent, giving him a furious look. He had nipped that little idea in the bud, and now she had no choice but to look out of the window, feeling as excluded herself as she had tried to make him feel.

The car sped out of St Petersburg, past the black statue of Lenin, past the first headquarters of the KGB, past the glittering gold onion domes of the churches and cathedrals.

Then they were out in the countryside.

Mile upon mile of flat, unkempt grassland stretched out like a green wilderness, and every now and then a set of vast concrete apartment buildings depressed the horizon. Train tracks ran along the road; trains carried salt and coal cargo in thick metal compartments.

Soon, they turned into the sunlit parks of Tsarskoe Selo.

It really was a private village.

A fairyland for the tsars of all the Russias.

Here, Catherine the Great had taken her lovers, here Empress Elizabeth had danced in the gold ballroom, here Tsar Nicholas had wintered with his family, and the Grand Duchesses Olga, Tatiana, Marie and Anastasia had skated on the frozen lake while the winter sunshine sparkled on the Chinese pagoda.

The car sped past the Alexander Palace, closed and empty, where the last Tsar was imprisoned with his family for five long months, and the yellow-white walls held terrible secrets... painful memories.

They turned a corner, and there stood imperial Russia in all its glory, the sun glinting on the gold turrets of the magnificent Catherine Palace.

It was vast, beautiful, a sky-blue Versailles with white pillars, carved gold turrets, golden statues, ornate gardens, a lake with fountains and summer-house and swans.

They parked the car under some trees.

'It's so wonderful to see it!' Natasha stared up into the piercing blue sky at the rich gold turrets. 'To think of Catherine the Great, young and beautiful, riding out in the green-gold uniform of the Preobrajensky, a true warrior queen and——'

'Not more history!' Dominic said unpleasantly, getting out of the car behind her and slamming the door.

She gave him a furious look. 'What exactly is the matter with you?'

'Nothing,' he bit out, and strode away towards the palace.

Xenia sighed, watching him walk away, tall and dark and bad-tempered. 'He's in such a bad mood all of a sudden. I can't think why—can you?'

'No,' Natasha said thickly, although she knew perfectly well why, and Xenia smiled slightly as they walked after him, along the ornate gardens of the palace, past gold statues and fountains and swans.

Touring the palace wasn't much fun, either.

Dominic's mood did not lift, and Natasha began to feel really hurt, shut out from him as he snapped at her, his eyes filled with dislike, biting out words with a mouth like a steel trap.

Even the sight of the fabled gold ballroom did not make Natasha feel any better, for she was more dazzled by Dominic than she ever could have been by the sight of all that gold blazing in the sunlight.

They drove home at three.

Dominic was hard-faced and silent, looking out of the window, tapping long fingers on his hard thigh as a sign that he was still angry with her, and she wanted him with simmering resentment, because this was the first time he had ever kept anger up and used it as a weapon against her, intending to inflict hurt.

When they got back to the hotel, Xenia and Natasha got out of the car, began to walk towards the steps of the hotel, and heard Dominic slamming the car door.

'I'm going for a walk,' he said tersely. 'I shan't bother to join you for lunch.'

Natasha turned to stare. 'What do you mean—you're going for a walk?'

'It's a fairly simple concept,' he bit out. 'You put the left foot down, and then the right.'

'But when will you be back?'

'When I feel like it.' Turning, he strode away down the street.

Natasha sped after him, and grabbed his arm. 'What's going on?' she demanded in a hurt, angry voice. 'Are you going to cancel the evening? Is the ballet off, just because you're in a bad temper?'

'And miss some of last night's action?' he drawled unpleasantly, eyes insulting. 'Not in a million years. I'll pick you up from the suite at six-thirty. In the meantime—shove off!'

Natasha gasped as he shook her hand from his arm and strode away without looking back, heading up the street towards the leafy statues of Artists' Square.

Fury exploded without warning in her. He's not getting away with speaking to me like that, she thought, hands clenching into fists and tears springing to her eyes.

She ran after him, heart thumping, and grabbed his arm again. 'How dare you treat me like this after everything that's happened between us? How *dare* you?'

'Never dare me, Natasha,' he drawled unpleasantly. 'You'll get more than you bargained for.'

'Don't threaten me, you swine!' she said hoarsely. 'I accepted that bargain with you because I wanted to see the ballet. But you're making me feel like some kind of tramp and I hate you for it. I hate you.'

'I can live with your hatred. I've lived with it for long enough, haven't I?'

Her mouth shook. 'I have feelings. You can't treat me like this and expect to get away with it. Don't you care that you're hurting me?'

'Not much!' he bit out, and shook her off again, crossing the road.

Natasha ran across the road after him, dodging traffic, tears burning her eyes. God, she was so furious, so filled with shaking emotion, that she could barely choke her words out. 'You have no right to speak to me like this!'

He ignored her, striding into Artists' Square, the statue of Pushkin with hand outstretched gleaming in the sunlight, trees lush green around the lawns while young lovers sat on benches, kissing, and artists sold paintings to tourists.

'You have no right!' Her voice was hoarse with anger and pain as she grabbed his arm again. 'No right to treat me like this, speak to me like this, make me feel——'

'Why?' he bit out, whirling on her, eyes blazing. 'You've been doing it to me since we first met!'

Natasha caught her breath, staring up into that hard, handsome face and realising suddenly how she would have felt if she had been in his shoes from the beginning, and appreciating for the first time the feelings he must have been put through, if he was genuine, in order to chase her as he had.

'Is that why you're angry?' she whispered, unable to believe he felt anything beyond desire for her.

'Well, what do you think? Look at the way you treated me this morning. Ignoring me, avoiding my kiss, giving me filthy looks after I'd offered you your dream evening on a silver platter!'

'With a heavy price, Dominic!'

'A price you're more than willing to pay.'

Her face flamed angrily. 'I can't help the way I feel about you physically. It's not my fault. Do you think I want to know I can't resist you?'

'There's no need to be so cold to me,' he ground out. 'Certainly not after making love with me last night, kissing me passionately this morning, accepting the tickets to the Kirov and agreeing to come to my room tonight—and then coming out of your bedroom with a face like ice and completely bloody ignoring me!'

Her eyes darted. 'I—I didn't think it would annoy you.'

'Well, that's cool,' he drawled unpleasantly. 'So long as I can use the same excuse and ignore you until we get to my bedroom tonight.'

'Oh, really?' She felt the pain deep in her heart. 'And you think I'll still go through with it, after this?'

'Do you want to go to the ballet or not?'

'You know I do!'

'Then you'll go through with it. Won't you?'

She breathed erratically, her heart racing with pain, eyes darting around wildly 'No! I can't, Dominic. I really want to go to the ballet, but I——'

'Don't want to come to my room?'

'Not if you're going to be sadistic to me.' Her voice trembled with hoarse emotion as she looked up at him, tears burning her eyes. 'Not if you're going to be cruel!'

'How can this be cruel?' he drawled sardonically, watching her face. 'You don't love me, do you? I mean— you're only mildly hurt, aren't you? It's not a terrible, unstoppable pain, is it? You're not actually *in love* with me, are you, Natasha?'

She couldn't look at him, breathing hard, emotion burning in her.

'Don't you avoid my eyes, you little bitch!' he bit out, eyes blazing with hatred. 'I'll make you answer me! Come on! I want to know. Do you have any feelings beyond sexual desire for me?'

Her breathing grew more erratic, her heart raced faster. 'No.' Her mouth was suddenly dry as ashes. She moistened her lips. 'I mean, yes.'

'Well, which is it, Natasha?' His eyes were hard. 'Yes or no? Do I mean anything at all to you, or not?'

'I...' She felt weak with fear suddenly, breathing faster, closing her eyes briefly, wishing she knew what to say, how to deal with this unexpected attack on her emotions. 'I...'

His eyes narrowed, a hard smile touched his mouth. 'Fine,' he said tightly, and turned on his heel, striding across the sunlit, leafy square.

'No, wait!' Natasha ran after him, weak with emotion, heart banging.

He turned, watching her coldly. 'Well?'

'I...' She struggled not to be this terrified of saying such a thing to a man who had already found his way into her obsessive, passionate heart and stamped his name all over it. 'I—I do care for you.'

His eyes softened, darkened, grew intense.

'I mean——' she could hear her voice shaking '—I care a little. I'm not saying I love you or anything serious, but I'm not just attracted to you sexually, and I'm not indifferent to you.'

There was a long, tense silence while she stared at the floor.

'Well,' Dominic said under his breath, 'that's a bit more like it.'

She looked up with dark, passionate eyes and asked thickly, 'Aren't you going to reciprocate, Dominic?'

'Not just at this moment,' he said coolly, a hard smile on his mouth.

Her face ran red with humiliation. 'My God...you swine! How dare you make me tell you something like that? How dare you just stand there and take it? How dare you not reciprocate in——?'

'I'm a free agent,' he said tightly. 'I can do what I like.'

'But you deliberately led me into saying that!' she said hoarsely. 'And now you're going to think I'm completely vulnerable to you, when all I did was——'

'Say a few words?' His eyes were angry. 'Yes, that's right. They disappeared as soon as you spoke. Just drifted off into the summer sunshine, as meaningless as they were empty.'

Her eyes blazed with hatred. 'They were not empty!'

'They're still gone,' he said harshly. 'And what are we left with?'

'I don't——'

'Actions, Natasha,' he bit out, his eyes dark. 'We're left with actions. And they speak a damned sight louder than words.'

Natasha just looked at him, eyes filled with confused and turbulent emotion, understanding what he was saying yet not believing it, refusing to believe it, especially after what he had just done.

Dominic watched her with narrowed eyes, reading the play of emotions on her face. A hard smile touched his handsome mouth. He nodded, as though satisfied by her pain.

'I'll see you at six-thirty,' he drawled, and turned on his heel, striding away from her across the square.

This time she did not follow him.

I'd rather die, she thought furiously, staring after him, than follow him. I'd rather have all my teeth pulled out by a maniac than ever chase after him again. I'd rather cut off my head and fry it in——

She broke off her enraged thoughts, turned on her heel and walked back across the busy street, back towards the hotel, struggling not to let her whirlwind emotions get the better of her.

In the suite, she went straight to her bedroom, needing privacy, locking the door and pacing up and down on the deep-pile carpet.

He only did all that because he knew I wanted to go to the Kirov and see *Swan Lake*. He did it because he knew I'd chase after him for that. He did it because he knew——

Her heart stopped beating with a sickening thud.

He knew she had begun to care for him.

I was right, then, she thought despairingly. He *did* start all this to see if he could make me fall madly in love with him. He thinks it'll be fun to bring me to my knees, make me not only go to bed with him but also give him my heart—no doubt it was a challenge to his male ego, especially given the life she had been leading for so long.

Then she thought of his parting shot: 'Actions speak a damned sight louder than words'.

And what have his actions been? she wondered.

But she already knew the answer to that.

They were the actions of a man obsessively in love.

She felt weak, suddenly, sinking down on to the bed, staring into space and feeling that obsessive passion rise up, clamouring inside her to get out, like a lioness in a diamond-studded collar, desperate for freedom, straining at the leash, ready to leap out in frenzied hunger for love and tear it to pieces . . .

I mustn't believe he loves me, she thought in panic. I can't cope if he does. I'll go over the edge, just topple into self-destruction.

For his actions made her want to believe he loved her. He had knocked Tony Kerr right out of her head, cleansed her of the humiliation he had left her with, broken open the sarcophagus she had been living in, and led her straight back to life with a vengeance...

'Actions speak louder than words,' she whispered to the four gilt-papered walls. 'Actions speak louder...'

His actions told her he loved her: deeply, passionately, obsessively.

But what if she was wrong?

What if she was wrong...?

CHAPTER EIGHT

AT SIX-THIRTY, she was ready and waiting for him, trembling with nerves as she stood in the living-room, the sun beginning to turn gold in the sky, glimmering on the spires of the city.

She had dressed with infinite care, her dark coffee-coloured lace dress both elegant and sexy, off the shoulder and fitted. He would love it, she knew that, and she had thought of his long hands unzipping it, peeling it from her body, even as she slid into it.

But more than that, she had thought of her struggle against the love she felt for him, that secret hothouse obsession, clamouring to get out, and how afraid she was of that, how terrified.

The doorbell rang, making her jump, gasping with excited panic.

'Ah!' Xenia laughed, eyes shining. 'Your handsome prince is here!'

Natasha shot her a brooding look, thinking of grand passions, of red-haired Russian beauties, and of handsome princes who deserted their obsessive lovers once the affair was over.

'Have a magical evening, darling.' Xenia kissed her cheek. 'I'll see you tomorrow...'

Natasha thanked her huskily and went out to the hall, opening the door to find Dominic towering over her, devastatingly handsome in a black dinner-jacket, his dramatic bone-structure and powerfully built body making her heart somersault with secret admiration.

'Are we leaving straight away?' she asked tightly, face proud.

'Only if you give me a kiss.' Dominic's eyes narrowed on her dark red mouth. 'And make it passionate, or I'll have to think about cancelling the ballet.'

Her temper flared at once. 'Why should I kiss you passionately after the way you treated me this afternoon?'

'OK, then,' he drawled, turning on his heel.

'Wait!' Furious, she ran after him, slamming the door of the suite and catching up with him along the corridor, breathing hard, green eyes flaring up at him angrily. 'All right! I'll kiss you!'

He laughed mockingly, waiting, and she was forced to stand on tiptoe in her high heels, wrapping her arms around his neck, kissing him as fiercely, angrily and passionately as she had the first day they had met, in his office in London.

The kiss was burningly exciting for them both.

He gave a rough exclamation of desire, grabbing her hips, pulling her body against him as the blood pulsed hotly through her, her mouth kissing his with a feel of erotic hatred.

'Oh, yes...!' he said thickly. 'You still know how to knock me for six with one kiss!'

'You really are despicable,' she whispered shakily, staring into his eyes, her heart pounding hard. 'I'm surprised you don't demand that I go to your bedroom right now in return for this night at the ballet!'

'Well, as I told you,' he said, tightly, 'actions speak a damned sight louder than words.'

Natasha studied him hotly through her lashes, her face flushed with desire, and felt as though she was being suspended by a thin wire of hope over a burning pit of destruction. One false move, just one, would send her into disaster. She must not believe he loved her. Must not...

'Yes...' Her voice was thick with emotion. 'Actions do speak louder. And what have your actions been? Relentless determination to get me into bed? No matter what you have to use as a levering weapon?'

His mouth tightened. 'Is that all you can say?'

'What else is there to say? You keep telling me you don't give a damn about me.'

'So I do,' he said, looking away, a muscle jerking in his cheek. Then he released her with a shove, pushing his hands into the pockets of his black trousers.

'Do you give a damn?' she whispered, half terrified by the question. 'Or is it all just——?'

'I don't even want to discuss it with you!' he said harshly, and took her wrist, striding along the corridor towards the lifts.

The car took them to the Mereyensky Palace.

The journey was tense. They both sat in the back, their bodies close and prickling with sexual awareness while emotions frazzled between them and their eyes watched each other secretly, hotly, obsessively.

It was a warm, beautiful night, and the streets were crowded with cars, coaches, buses—all unloading people at the doors to the Kirov, that legendary home of Russia's greatest artform, ballet.

The car dropped them at the entrance, too, and Dominic led Natasha into the theatre as cars beeped, traffic jammed, and a vast hubbub of chattering people milled around the open doors.

'Nijinsky,' Dominic said tersely beside her, and pointed with a long finger to the wall inside the foyer, where a stone frieze of Nijinsky as a faun gleamed under the chandeliers.

Natasha looked at it with witch-green eyes, her face white and taut with emotion, her thoughts entirely on Dominic.

'For God's sake, don't sulk,' he muttered thickly, staring at her. 'You'll ruin the evening for yourself if you do.'

'Why should you care if I do or not?'

'Because I had to practically break my neck to get these tickets at such short notice.'

'For my benefit?' she asked rawly. 'Or your own?'

His eyes flashed. 'Must you be so determined to believe the worst of me?'

'Oh, pardon me! But aren't you the one who demanded I come to your bedroom tonight in exchange for my night out at the ballet?'

'And I still demand it,' he drawled with a tight smile. 'But that shouldn't stop you enjoying the Kirov. It's the one place in all Russia that really belongs to you, and we both know it. Why do you think I went to so much trouble to get these tickets? Especially for *Swan Lake*. You're lucky they're performing it while we're here, let alone to have front-row tickets for it.'

Her eyes scanned his face as wild hope burned her heart. 'If you really did it for me, why is there a price-tag attached?'

'It's not such a bad price-tag, Natasha!' he bit out, dark red colour staining his cheekbones. 'I realise you're still scared, but don't tell me you won't enjoy it, because I know damned well that you will!'

At once, she looked away, heat burning her cheeks and emotion tearing at her heart. Everything was going badly wrong between them. Just the sight of him was beginning to burn her so deeply that she couldn't bear to look at him, talk to him, clamouring for his love like this and not getting it.

Dominic gave an angry sigh, took her wrist, said tightly, 'Oh, the hell with it! Let's take our seats before the performance starts.'

She allowed him to lead her inside the theatre itself, and her eyes softened a little as she saw the beauty, the gold covering every wall, every box, every inch of the legendary Kirov, with its blue velvet seats and curtains the perfect foil for all that glittering gold.

Here, they had all danced, all the greats in Russian ballet throughout history, from Nijinsky to Nureyev, Pavlova to Kchessinska, Balanchine to Baryshnikov.

And my great-grandmother was among them, Natasha thought, as she sat in the front row beside Dominic.

'A smile at last!' Dominic drawled sardonically beside her. 'Let me guess what you're thinking of. Your great-grandmother.'

Natasha couldn't help smiling up at him, her green eyes glittering with strange, hypnotic lights. 'She must have been so proud, dancing here on this stage, alongside Kchessinska and Pavlova.'

'She was certainly beautiful,' he agreed with a cool drawl, but he leaned his dark head close to her, a smile on his tough mouth. 'After seeing her photograph, I can quite understand why her prince loved her.'

'He didn't stay with her, though,' Natasha said rawly, her eyes intent on his handsome face.

'Surely that was because of the revolution?'

'No, he left her before that. Don't forget, her daughter was born in 1913, four years before the revolution.'

The blue eyes watched her closely.

'It was just a love affair to him. But she fell wildly in love. It was her grand passion, and she never stopped loving him, not even on her deathbed.'

'Grand passion...' he murmured, eyes narrowing. 'Or obsessive love?'

'Both are equally dangerous.'

His eyes grew dark, almost black, and suddenly he drawled, 'Tell me, Natasha—did anyone in your family ever compare you with your great-grandmother? When you were a little girl, I mean? A small child?'

'Always. I grew up knowing I was just like her. In fact, I can't remember a time when I didn't know that I was her double.'

'Her double. I see.' He watched her intently. 'And Tony Kerr was your first boyfriend, wasn't he? A boyfriend who never made love to you.'

'You know he was!'

'Your only boyfriend, in fact?'

Her eyes flared. 'That's right!'

'And what was your first thought on meeting him? Or when love sprang up inside you? What was your first thought?'

'I sensed terrible danger.'

'But surely that would only be natural in the circumstances?'

'What circumstances?' she asked thickly, but of course she knew, suddenly, saw it in the mirror of his dark eyes, so intense, so obsessive, so like her.

It wasn't Tony who had made her terrified of love.

It was her mother.

Fear had been bred in her, from the cradle, by her unwitting mother, who had seen the resemblance in her green-eyed, red-haired, passionate daughter from the start, and had been frightened by it, frightened for her future, frightened by her all-consuming capacity to love.

It's coloured my whole life, Natasha realised in horror. It drew me into that mess with Tony, smashed up my life in Kent, brought me to London, locked me away for years without love...

Dominic was watching the rapid play of emotion on her face, the pain and shock in her eyes, the taut white beauty of her features starkly etched by appalled recognition of her whole emotional life.

'I doubt she knew what she was doing,' Dominic said deeply. 'She seemed a calm, rather serene woman to me. Very unlike you in temperament. I expect she was just afraid for you.'

Natasha stared at him in shock. 'When did you realise it was her?'

'Just now. Same as you.' A hard smile touched his mouth. 'Perhaps a few minutes before...'

The lights slowly began to die. The orchestra began to play the opening strains of Tchaikovsky's *Swan Lake*.

Music swelled in tragedy and romance, filling her heart with love for her great-grandmother, for herself, for Dominic, and for the right to be capable of grand passion at its most extreme.

The curtain rose, and the ballet began to unfold on stage.

Prince Siegfried fell heavily in love with Odette, the beautiful young woman turned into a swan by the Enchanter. Natasha felt the tragedy touch her heart.

And the tragedy was that the spell was never broken—Odette remained a swan, Siegfried married Odile, and death came to claim Odette instead of life, love, freedom...

She never broke the spell, Natasha thought, staring intently at the beautiful ballerina. She never broke the spell.

When the curtain fell on the first act and the lights went up, she was still thinking over and over, repeating obsessively in her mind: she never broke the spell.

'Let's go for a drink,' Dominic drawled, and as his hand curled over her wrist she was already standing, watching him with hot, dark, possessive eyes, thinking, He's helped me break the spell, he's helped me, he's helped me...

Actions speak louder than words.

Her heart lurched as she looked back over his actions, saw each one leading to this moment, meticulously breaking each link in the chain which had imprisoned her all her life, not just for four years, but forever, forever, since she was a child, afraid of love, afraid of herself, afraid of her great-grandmother's face staring back at her from the mirror.

Dominic had broken all that for her, and he had done it because he loved her. Deeply. Passionately. Obsessively.

I'm in love with him, she realised with a sickening lurch of the heart, but as the fear washed over her in waves, she reminded herself that he must love her to have done all of this, he must love her, he *must*...

And if he does love me, she thought fiercely, then it's all right to love him, it can't be dangerous, because he'll stay with me, match my hunger, my passionate obsession, my fathomless capacity for love...

The fear disappeared as though in a puff of smoke.

He loves me, she thought incredulously, as they went up the echoing marble stairs.

He loves me, and his love has broken the spell, because not only do I know where my fear of love really comes from, but I no longer need to fear it if he loves me too!

They were walking into a vast deep-carpeted room, huge chandeliers glittering in the ceiling, and Natasha wanted to stop him, get him alone, kiss him until they both lost their minds, go to bed, make wild love with him, lose herself in his body—and tell him that she loved him.

'Here.' He handed her a drink.

'Dominic . . .!' she whispered intently, staring at him with her strange obsessive green eyes, hot and dark and filled with blazing emotion.

'What?' He stared down at her. 'What is it?'

'Dominic, I——' she began hoarsely, ready to let the words and the emotions spill out of her.

'Dominic!' a female voice behind her said in shock.

Natasha froze, terror knifing through her as she spun, her face white as snow, to stare at the ravishing blonde beauty behind her.

'Kyra . . .?' Dominic's voice was like acid in her heart as she turned back to stare at him, saw his face rigid with shock, his blue eyes blazing with some primitive emotion.

'My God, is it really you?' Kyra stepped towards him with a smile, and she really was beautiful, small and slender, blonde hair pulled back in an elegant chignon, her face fine-boned, her blue eyes dazzling.

'Imagine bumping into you here, of all places!' Dominic bent his dark head, kissed her mouth.

Natasha sucked in her breath, wanting to stab him through the heart, stab her through the heart, appalled by the emotions tearing at her in savage order—jealousy, betrayal, hatred, despair, murderous rage and indescribable pain.

He still loved her.

He still loved Kyra.

They were standing talking, laughing, his hand on her slim shoulder and her eyes blazing up into his with love, admiration, respect.

Oh, my God, she thought in horror—and I nearly told him I was in love with him. I nearly made a colossal fool of myself. Nearly went over the brink into what I've feared all along.

'Have you met Natasha?' Dominic was saying coolly, turning to her. 'Darling—this is Kyra, an old friend of mine. Kyra, this is Natasha Carne.'

'How do you do?' Kyra looked at her with a haughty smile.

Natasha's face was blazing with hatred and jealousy. 'Hello.'

'How long are you both in town for?' Kyra turned back to Dominic with a dismissive flick of her lashes, making Natasha want to claw her eyes out, chop them into tiny pieces, serve them with fresh caviare for lunch.

'Just another week,' drawled Dominic, hands thrust in black trouser pockets, one long leg bent as he ran his blue eyes over Kyra's beautiful face and body. 'And you?'

'A year,' Kyra drawled with her seductively Russian accent. 'I missed home so much, I just had to come back. Why don't we get together while you're here, talk about old times?'

'That would be fun,' Dominic said lazily, making Natasha stare at him with secret murderous jealousy. 'I'll try to look you up, give you a call before we leave.'

'You're staying at the Europe?'

'That's right.' The bell rang for the second act, and he bent his dark head for another kiss from Kyra's pale pink Russian mouth. 'See you soon, perhaps...' He turned to Natasha, put his strong hand at her back, and drawled, 'Come on, darling. Mustn't miss the grand finale.'

Natasha didn't say goodbye to Kyra. She didn't trust herself not to stick a fork in her beautiful blonde head.

Allowing Dominic to lead her back into the glittering gold theatre, she was appalled by her own savage jealousy, and the pain that clawed at her heart as she thought of her own doomed love.

'That was a shock,' Dominic murmured as they took their seats in the front row. 'I can't believe she's here.'

'I bet not!' she said savagely, hating him.

'What's the——?' Then he broke off, dark lashes flickering, a smile touching his handsome mouth. 'Is this jealousy talking, my darling?'

'Don't flatter yourself!' she said thickly, choking on the words.

'You can't lie to me about something so obvious,' he said softly, eyes mocking her. 'I can see it in your face. And you were about to tell me something important, weren't you, before she appeared?'

'I certainly shan't be telling you now!' Natasha's hoarse voice and blazing, passionate eyes made several people turn in their seats near by to stare as she sat there, shaking with emotion. 'If anything, I'm glad she's turned up out of the blue like this. It'll give you someone else to pursue to the bedroom and leave me alone!'

'Don't be so stupid. I don't want her. I want you!'

'Well, you can't have me, so I suggest you ring her up and——'

'I damned well won't!' he bit out thickly, his hand clamping down over hers, fingers hurting her. 'Or have you forgotten the bargain we made? You'll come to my bedroom directly after the ballet, or I'll——'

'Or what?' she demanded. 'We're here now. What can you do to stop me welshing on the deal?'

His eyes narrowed as he drawled tightly, 'I can be cruel to you, Natasha. I can be so cruel to you for the next week that you'll end up on your knees, begging me to make love to you, begging me to forgive you.'

Natasha went white, looking away at once, aware deep inside that he could tear her to pieces easily, just as he had done this afternoon when he got his emotional revenge in Artists' Square, forcing her to tell him she cared for him, then walking away without a backward glance.

'So...' he drawled softly beside her, 'what's it to be? Keep the bargain or face the consequences?'

Her mouth shook. 'I'll keep the bargain. But it's only for fifteen minutes—remember? And I'll kill you rather than stay in that room for a second longer.'

'Don't worry,' he said mockingly. 'I'm a faster mover under pressure. I'll have you right where I want you before you know what's hit you.'

The lights went down as Natasha looked away from him, shaking with emotion.

How could she fight him? He outfoxed her at every step, no matter what she tried to do, and he always had done, always would. It had made her love him, and now she was lost, hopelessly, unable to stop the process he had set in motion when he first looked into her eyes, in that lift, and made her heart start spinning.

Tchaikovsky's music filled the theatre, the doomed love-story of Odette and Siegfried reaching its tragic climax.

Nothing matters to me any more, Natasha thought. Nothing but Dominic and needing his love. Everything else had fallen away from her now, all the old wounds, the old fears, and as the curtain fell on *Swan Lake*, so it fell on the past for Natasha, finally and forever.

Applause erupted in the Kirov, the dancers took endless curtain-calls, roses were thrown on stage, and the prima ballerina was treated like a goddess.

When the applause died down, the lights went back up and Dominic got to his feet, looking down at her with hard, narrowed eyes.

'You can't postpone it forever,' he drawled. 'Unless you want to take up residence, here in the theatre, and stay here for the rest of your life.'

Natasha flushed, getting to her feet. 'I can delay it.'

'That will only whet my appetite.' His strong hand curled possessively around her wrist.

People spilled out of the Kirov, on to the night-time streets of St Petersburg. Traffic zoomed and beeped along the streets and the squares. French lamps glowed white against the trees; the air was cool and crisp.

Natasha froze as she saw Kyra, blonde and beautiful, getting into the front of a Mercedes parked at the kerb. She turned, saw Dominic and Natasha, and waved at Dominic.

'*Dosvedenya*!'

Dominic raised a strong hand in greeting, smiling. 'Bye...'

'I'll give you a call!' Kyra got into the car, slammed the door shut, and it took off immediately, red tail-lights flashing.

Natasha felt sick inside, watching their own car come gliding up to collect them, and as she got into the luxurious rear beside Dominic, she couldn't stop the jealousy eating at her like acid.

The car sped back to their hotel.

'I suppose you'll be taking her out to dinner tomorrow night, will you?' Natasha heard her jealous voice ask.

'Would you care if I did?' he drawled, shooting her a brooding look through those heavy eyelids.

'No, I told you—I'll be glad if you chase her instead of me.'

'And you're not jealous?'

'Not in the slightest.' Her voice shook even as she spoke.

He smiled tightly. 'So you're not interested in how it felt for me to see her again?'

'No,' she said automatically, but her eyes flashed to his with dark, secret jealousy, wishing she could retract that no and demand to hear how he had felt.

'OK, then. I shan't tell you.'

Her mouth tightened and she looked away again. The gold dome of St Isaac's looked so beautiful in the moonlight that she was sorry it blurred as her eyes sheened with hot tears.

'You have only to ask,' Dominic said coolly beside her.

Pride warred with jealousy. Jealousy won. 'All right, then!' She turned back to look at him in the dark interior. 'Tell me how you felt when you saw her again.'

'Sure you want to hear?'

'Of course I'm sure!'

'Well, why should it interest you if you're not jealous?'

'Why should my relationship with Tony have interested you?' she countered tightly. 'If *you* weren't jealous?'

'Because I knew it would help me get you into bed,' he drawled mockingly. 'But I don't really see where your interest in Kyra comes into it. Unless, of course, you're hiding your jealousy from me out of pride.'

'Are you going to tell me how you felt or not?'

He smiled lazily, watching her in silence.

Her eyes flashed. 'I'm not going to beg!'

'No, you're not going to beg. Not yet,' he drawled, smiling angrily. 'But you will later tonight when I make love to you.' His hand slid over her thigh, making shivers of pleasure and excitement flood her. 'And afterwards—I promise I'll tell you how it felt to see Kyra again.'

Fury rose like lava in her mind. 'My God, you swine!'

He laughed softly as the car drew up outside the Hotel Europe. 'Ah, here we are. Home at last. Come on—you have another date with destiny to keep!'

Natasha was trembling with rage as she got out of the car, unable to believe he could be so damned cruel to her, tricking her into revealing her jealousy and the deep need she had to know what had run through his heart and mind when he saw Kyra again, for the first time in years.

They both knew already how she would feel if she saw Tony. If any emotion rose in her for that long-forgotten rat, it would be pity. His hold on her was as dead as her love for him, and her sense of humiliation.

But Kyra was a very different matter. And Natasha desperately needed to know how Dominic had felt. He knew it, too, the swine, and was going to use it as another lever to force her into making love with him.

He can go to hell, she thought savagely, as they walked into the marble foyer and went straight to the lifts. I'd rather die than let him touch me.

Dominic laughed softly as they rode up in the lift together. 'Oh, look at those eyes! You really hate my guts, don't you?'

'Must you treat me like this?' she demanded thickly.

'How do I treat you, Natasha?'

'As though I have no feelings.'

'You're not the only one with feelings,' he said tersely, 'as I believe I made clear this afternoon.'

The lift doors slid open, and he took her wrist, possessive as always, striding along the corridor to his suite.

'Don't try to make it look,' she said tightly, 'as though I've hurt any feelings you have for me, because I know you don't have any.'

'Oh, you know that, do you?' He opened the door to the suite angrily. 'What are you—psychic?'

Natasha hesitated in the doorway, staring at his face with hot green eyes. 'What are you saying, Dominic? That you do care?'

'Of course I care!' he bit out under his breath, and pushed her into the hallway, slamming the door behind him, punching on the light and throwing his key on the telephone table. 'Look at the trouble I've gone to to get you!'

'But you only want me in your bed!' she said fiercely.

'Yes, and I'm going to get you there,' he bit out tightly. 'Right now!'

She gasped as he took her hand, strode angrily to the bedroom, kicked open the door and dragged her in after him, not bothering with the light, just pulling her over to the bed with him.

CHAPTER NINE

'DON'T...!' she cried out hoarsely, struggling, but he was too strong for her, throwing her on to the bed even while she fought him, and as she landed with a thud in the darkness, the only thing she could see were his glittering, savage eyes.

'Your fifteen minutes starts now!' he said harshly, and then his mouth closed over hers.

Natasha continued to fight, but his response was to press her down into the pillows, trap her wrists with his hands, her kicking legs with his powerful thighs, and to silence any screams she might have made by kissing her hard, bruising her lips while she sobbed and struggled beneath him.

'Please!' she moaned against his mouth. 'Don't hurt me any more...'

He tensed, raising his head, face darkly flushed. 'Any more?' He was breathing hard. 'But this is the first time I've ever really hurt you. Isn't it?'

She looked away with a sob, tears burning her eyes.

'Natasha?' His strong hand took her chin, forced her to look at him. 'Well? Have I ever hurt you like this before?'

'No...' she was forced to admit shakingly.

'Then what did you mean?'

Her heart twisted as she struggled to find the words, afraid she would break down in tears at any moment, too scared to let this continue in case he made full love to her and devastated her with the crushing emptiness of sex without love.

'Answer me!' His voice thickened with angry emotion. 'How have I hurt you before?'

Her mouth trembled and she obstinately shook her head, burning inside with love-hate.

'Answer me, damn you!' he bit out hoarsely, and the tone of his voice made her catch her breath, staring up into his flushed face, seeing the fierce emotion glittering in his eyes.

'I...' She wanted so badly to tell him the truth that she found it even more difficult than it should have been.

'Yes?' His eyes desperately scanned her face in the darkness. 'Yes? Tell me!'

Fear and anger rose in her. 'Go to hell, Dominic! I'd rather die than tell you how I feel!'

His mouth tightened. 'Die, then!' he bit out thickly, lowering his dark head. 'But die with pleasure...' and his mouth closed hotly over hers, making her moan against her will, hands on his broad shoulders as she tried to push him away, but that kiss kept dragging her back to him, back into the whirlpool of passion they shared in such hot, secret, obsessive privacy.

Her mouth opened beneath his, and her arms wrapped around his neck, hating him, loving him, kissing him feverishly, her fingers stroking his dark hair, his throat, moving around to his tough jaw, running along it like a blind woman hungry for every inch of him.

Their bodies twisted in angry excitement on the bed. His hands moved up to her breasts, caressing them while she moaned dazedly, licking his lips with her tongue, fumbling with the black tie at his neck, tearing it off as her desire became blind, uncaring, all-powerful...

'Oh, God!' Dominic said shakingly, and unzipped the coffee lace dress, sliding it down over her bare shoulders, watching her breasts bounce free, nipples hardened with excitement and aching for his touch.

'I hate you!' she whispered hoarsely, and moaned as he cupped her bare breasts. 'Oh, yes...yes...!'

Dominic gave a rough exclamation of desire, his mouth burning down over hers, fondling her breasts with angry hands, his hard body moving against hers with a primitive, sexual rhythm as the emotional lines of communication between them began to frazzle savagely, and their lovemaking became tainted by dark, hungry obsession.

Sweat dewed her lashes, she was on fire, hating him, burning for him, and her hatred was strong enough to make her fingers unbutton his shirt as though punishing him with desire, tearing at the buttons, pushing it off savagely, running her hands with angry hatred over his bare chest.

'Hate me, do you?' he whispered raggedly against her tongue.

'Yes, I hate you!' Her hands moved savagely over his naked spine, down to the taut buttocks and hard thighs. 'I hate you!'

He groaned hoarsely. His hands began to tug at her dress, bunched around her waist, and Natasha cried out with helpless excitement as she felt her dress being pulled angrily down over her slim hips and thighs, making her wriggle to help him get it off.

Naked save for silk briefs, she welcomed him back to her with hungry hands and mouth, letting him slide between her thighs, his hands moving at once to her bare breasts while she kissed him feverishly.

Prickles of fury ran along her scalp, her skin, making her jaw tense with excitement and the need to release what she felt, no matter how, because she couldn't stand the tension any more, just couldn't bear it...

'I'd like to kill you!' she said hoarsely, kissing him, running her hands over his body.

'I hope you mean that!' he bit out, breathing heavily, his skin on fire and his heart thundering above her.

'You sadistic swine! You're enjoying my hatred, aren't you?'

'Every last drop! It's the only real emotional response you've ever given me, and I'm going to wallow in it!'

She moaned as his fingers slid her briefs off, down her slim thighs, enjoying her angry, excited writhing as she let him strip her naked again, clearly at the end of her tether, unable to hold out any more against him, wanting him too much to be able to stop.

'Want me to touch you?' he asked thickly, running his skilful fingers up and down her inner thighs, taunting her with her own desire, lightly brushing the wet, wet flesh that clamoured for his touch.

'Yes, yes...' she moaned insanely.

'Say please!'

'Go to hell!' she shouted savagely.

'Say it!'

She tried to resist, but as his finger teasingly brushed her hot, wet flesh again she heard her tortured voice moan, 'Please...!' and then she cried out in satisfaction as his finger touched her firmly at last, sliding inside her slowly and remaining motionless, making her rock against his palm, eyes tightly shut, hoarse moans of delicious excitement coming from her throat.

Hatred was so close to love, such a fine line separating the two, and Natasha was blind with both now, completely out of her mind with emotion, the need to express it in some way, physically or with words.

The thought of going back to her room alone to cry in jealous despair was too much for her.

She'd had enough. She couldn't take any more. She refused to be lonely and scared and locked up *any more*.

Her nude body rocked against his palm in blind need, and it felt so freeing just to let it all happen, lying here like this, her thighs spread wantonly for the man she loved...

And she needed so badly to express her feelings. She felt as though she'd been living behind a stone dam for years, all her life, and that it was crumbling down under the onslaught of obsessive love and desire.

Let it crumble, she thought angrily.

Let it go.

If Dominic didn't love her, at least she would have this night, this moment, this unleashing of all the violent cross-currents of emotion she felt for him.

At least she would have taken a stand instead of hiding away from life. At least she would have demanded her rights as a woman, to love, to hate, and to give her body the satisfaction it craved.

'Take me!' her low, shaking voice said against his hungry mouth. 'Take me now!'

The atmosphere tilted between them as Dominic drew harsh, rapid breaths, his heart hammering, then withdrew his hand to fumble with his trousers, and this time when the zip flared down Natasha didn't try to stop him.

He came back to her naked, and she almost went berserk with desire, gasping hoarsely, repeatedly, panting as their nude bodies met and twisted together for the first time.

'Yes...yes...' she pleaded as she felt the hot, hard press of his manhood against her aching, slippery flesh.

He entered her.

The savage moan of painful satisfaction she gave as their bodies joined made even her hair stand on end as the thought ricocheted in her mind—'woman wailing for her demon lover'.

She felt the pain gnaw and tear at her but, God, it was satisfying, and yes, it was delicious, and soon, very soon it faded into intense excitement as she moved her hips wantonly, her naked body spread out with blazing sexual hunger, freedom making her provocative as she relished the thick hard flesh inside her and the satisfaction of feeling it fill her.

'Tell me you hate me!' Dominic bit out.

Her eyes blazed hot, obsessive, dark with love-hate and desire, and she whispered her hatred to him as he rocked against her body, enjoying her guttural moans of sexual excitement.

So this was what it felt like. 'Real...' she whispered hoarsely, clutching his naked buttocks with wanton hands. 'So real...'

He watched her in dazed intoxication as she drove against him for her own satisfaction.

She moved faster, faster, her breathing turning to hoarse agony, her jaw tensing and her thighs going rigid and her eyes closing tightly at the approach of orgasm.

It exploded in delicious black ecstasy, like a giant hand wrenching her centre and shaking out all the anger, hatred and despair of her whole life, releasing it in violent spasm of pleasure while she screamed savagely and felt saliva run out of her mouth over her protruding tongue.

For those seconds, she sounded like a ragged, dehumanised animal. Then, all at once, she collapsed, spent, her eyes still rolled up, her tongue lolling over her wet lips, dragging air into her lungs.

Dominic was staring down at her, his face contorted as though he might die with agonised pleasure, and when he was sure she had subsided, he began to drive for his own satisfaction, gripping her hips, slamming into her.

Freedom rippled through her as she felt his body thundering into her own. She moaned softly in delicious exhaustion, spreading out for him, loving every second of it, until he gave a hoarse shout of ecstasy and she was able to watch his eyes roll back, his body jerk and shudder, growls of thick pleasure coming from his throat.

He fell on her, dragging air into his lungs, and his face against her throat was burning as though he had a temperature of 103. She felt waves of tenderness for him, sliding her arms around him, kissing his shoulder again and again and again.

All the hatred had gone now, and the anger. Strange how sex could expunge those feelings, leaving only the good and gentle emotions, like love and tenderness and sorrow.

Tears stung her eyes without warning.

Oh, God, don't let me cry, she thought, closing her eyes tight as her mouth began to shake and emotion flooded into her heart like a rip-tide, building suddenly and without warning, unstoppable as the tears burst from her eyes and streamed hotly down her cheeks.

Don't let him see you cry, she thought fiercely, and bit her lip, fighting her own tears in the darkness while the man she loved recovered in her arms.

'Darling,' he murmured suddenly, raising his dark head, 'I really——'

Her breath sucked in painfully, hoarse emotion in that one shaking breath, tears falling freely down her cheeks as she turned her face from him, trying to hide.

'You're crying!' He stared, immobile. 'Darling, please——'

'Let's not pretend, Dominic!' she whispered rawly. 'You don't love me any more than I love you! This happened between us because I couldn't resist you any more, and you weren't prepared to waste any more time on me.'

'That's not true, Natasha,' he said deeply. 'Why must you always read the worst into me? I made love to you because you asked me to.'

'Don't tell me you would have taken a refusal tonight, because I don't believe you!'

'I'm not a rapist!' he said hoarsely. 'What do you think I would have done? Forced you against your will? Don't be absurd, Natasha. If I haven't done that until now, why should I suddenly change?'

Her eyes filled with more tears as she whispered, 'Kyra?'

He gave a deep sigh, but he smiled, bending his head to kiss away her tears. 'Darling, I can't believe you're still going on about her. Do you really think I'd be here like this with you if I——?'

'Look, I'm a big girl!' she said, not wanting to hear how much he would prefer to be with Kyra, and desperate to prove that she didn't love him as deeply and obsessively as she very definitely did. 'I can take it if our lovemaking isn't going to lead to anything. I can take it if we just say goodbye, now, and go our separate——'

'Is that what you want?' he demanded, eyes flaring with sudden anger.

She looked at him, her mouth shaking. 'Isn't it what you want?'

'No!'

Hope flared in her heart, turning her eyes molten with love. 'But if all you ever wanted from me was sex...?'

He was silent for a moment, his body tense and his eyes veiled by those heavy eyelids. Then he drawled tightly, 'I told you once that I didn't think I'd ever tire of you. That still stands true. I want to make love to you for a very long time to come, Natasha. You're the most exciting lover I've ever had, and I want much, much more of you than just one night.'

Her heart crashed to the ground, shattering into a thousand tiny pieces, making her feel desolate. Suddenly, their lovemaking seemed like a colossal mistake, a terrible disaster.

He really doesn't love me, she thought in despair, staring into his flushed, sweat-hot face. But I love him. I love him with everything I've got, and I can never tell him about it, never let him see it, never share it with him.

Not only that, but I'll never stop loving him.

Fear turned her face white as snow, her eyes great green pools of emotion against that stark porcelain skin, and she looked into the future, saw her doomed love echoing the tragedy of Odette...

For she would carry on loving him obsessively, making love with him in agonising excitement, and then when the affair was over, when he tired of her, she would have to carry on working with his mother, seeing him all the time, living for her brief glimpses of him, loving him for eternity, as trapped and chained up by her love for him as she had been trapped and chained up by the past.

It was an intolerable vision of an intolerable future after such an intolerable past.

She looked at his face and knew she had to be brave, had to be strong, had to keep her dignity this time, not let herself be used and humiliated by a man who did not love her, regardless of her feelings for him.

'OK,' she said with a tense smile, and lied, for the first time with her eyes, not letting them glow with love for him. 'I can't pretend that making love with you wasn't the most incredible and exciting experience of my life. And you know I can't resist you, so I shan't argue with you. I'll just have to accept that this is how we feel about each other. And make the best of it.'

Dominic stared at her as though she'd stuck a knife in him, and as the colour receded from his face he flicked his gaze away from her, frowning deeply, staring fixedly at nothing.

'But I'm so tired, darling,' Natasha whispered, aware she would burst into tears again if she stayed much longer with him. 'It's been a long day for us both.'

He was breathing rapidly, his eyes darting.

'Would you mind if I went to my own room now?' she asked huskily, kissing his shoulder. 'It's very late and——'

'Yes, I would mind!' he said thickly, his dark head swinging back to look at her with fierce, glittering eyes. 'I want to make love to you again.'

'No! Dominic, I——'

'Shut up!' he bit out hoarsely, his mouth shaking, and then bent his head to kiss her angrily as his body stirred inside her, hard and pulsing with new life, his long hands moving with hatred over her breasts, her thighs.

'Don't...' she whispered as the tears came again. 'Please...'

He kissed her deeper, and she started to cry softly against his mouth, tears streaming down her cheeks, agony tearing at her heart just at the thought of making love with him again in these terrible circumstances.

'I can't...' Her voice was shaking with emotion, so much emotion that he stopped kissing her and raised his head, eyes black, to stare down at her.

For a second, they just lay there, still coupled and naked, each in their own private hell.

Then Dominic said, 'Will you tell me why you're crying?'

'I don't know why,' she lied. 'I—I think it's just the shock of making love for the first time. Can't you understand that?'

His face flushed darker red. 'Yes...of course...forgive me.'

'I—I need time to get used to the physical shock, and the exhaustion. It's made me emotional...'

He gave a harsh nod, his eyes jet-black now as he stared at her, the emotions in those eyes quite primitive. 'Very well. Go back to your own room. I don't want to make love to someone who's crying like this. It's too boring.'

She flinched, but he didn't notice because he was too busy withdrawing from her body.

'Go on, go to bed,' he drawled, and flung himself on to his back. 'I'll see you in the morning.'

Natasha felt as though she had been physically beaten up, but she had started this pretence, so she had to go on with it, didn't she?

Trying not to scream with the terrible pain she felt in her heart, she slid naked out of bed, trembling as she pulled her dress on, zipped it up, while Dominic watched her in angry silence.

I'll never see him again, she thought in despair, and stopped suddenly to stare at him with dark hunger.

I want to memorise every inch of his face, she thought, her eyes glimmering strangely in the darkness. If I'm going to love him in secret for the rest of my life, I need to stamp him in my mind, just as he is now, his black hair tousled from my touch, blue eyes glittering so fiercely with dark emotion, a flush of anger on those rough-hewn cheekbones, and a tough sulky look to his handsome mouth.

'Goodnight,' she whispered, as tears filled her eyes.

'Must you make it so damned impersonal?' he demanded thickly, emotion flashing hard and black in his eyes. 'We've just made love! Come here and give me a goodnight kiss!'

She did, sinking down on the bed beside him, staring at him with obsessive love, one slender white hand tracing the harsh contours of that dramatic Russian face.

Then she bent her head and kissed him passionately, fiercely, her eyes closed tight as though to savour this brief feeling of love when there was no love, and no future.

'Natasha...!' he whispered hoarsely, and pulled her down on to the bed beside him, his mouth closing with fierce, almost desperate passion on hers as his hands tangled in her hair.

She moaned in despair, but she clung desperately to him, her mouth open, hungry, matching his kiss with a fervour that was unsurpassed.

He raised his head, darkly flushed, staring down at her with eyes like hot blue fire. 'Stay! Stay with me to-night, Natasha.'

'I can't!' she whispered in agony.

'Please.' He framed her face with his strong, shaking hands. 'I can't bear letting you leave like this.'

'I can't bear having to leave,' she said hoarsely, clinging to him. 'But I must, Dominic. I must...'

His mouth tightened and shook. 'Fine! The hell with you!'

She flinched, her face white.

'Go on!' he blazed savagely. 'Get out of my sight!'

Tears slid over her lashes. She ran from the bed, blind with tears as she stumbled out of the room, fumbled with the front door and let herself out into the corridor.

How can I live with this pain? she thought, trembling with the key in her hand, letting herself back into her own suite, barely able to see the lock or the door-handle, everything blurring into a hot mist before her eyes.

I'll just have to get used to it, she realised in agony. Chasing after him won't do any good. I learned that last time. But, oh God, how can I live with it...?

The suite was silent, and Natasha tried not to make any noise as she went into her bedroom, tears still streaming down her face, and took her suitcase from beside the wardrobe.

It took her three hours to pack. She was crying so hard that she had to stop every now and then, defeated by waves of emotion, lying down on the bed with her hands over her face, crying until she thought she would die from it.

And, of course, she didn't sleep.

CHAPTER TEN

DAWN light crept over St Petersburg. Natasha looked out at the golden spires, shimmering softly in the blue-grey-gold morning air.

The desk in front of her was covered with half-written, tear-stained letters. At first, she had tried to explain why she was leaving and why he must never follow her. But her words were too emotional, and she was afraid of making such a fool of herself, especially to him, the man she loved and respected. This was something she could live with only if she behaved, at the end, with great dignity. It felt like mounting a scaffold for execution. One could only accept the unacceptable and display quiet faith.

But I can't just leave without telling him how I feel, she realised, because that would be unjust. He had done so much for her. Changed her life in so many ways, healing old wounds, moving her into a future she had been unprepared for, and teaching her so much about life that she knew she would never be the same again.

Dominic had been a swine to her, but he had also been good, and he deserved more than silent desertion.

So in the end, she just wrote: 'I'm in love with you.'

She sat staring at it for a long time. There was no need to address or sign it. He could hardly think it came from anyone else, certainly not if she left it on her pillow, sealed in an envelope, with his name written on the front of it.

He would probably smile, or at least feel triumphant when he read it. But he knew all about her past, and he knew how dangerous love was in her mind, how very frightened she was by it, how unable to cope. He would know what she was trying to say—that if he had any humanity at all, he would not try to follow her.

Time was moving on, though, and she had to make sure she could get out of the country now, today. So she rang British Airways' London office and was lucky enough to get the last seat on the eleven o'clock flight from St Petersburg to London.

It was seven o'clock in the morning now, and she had to get out of this suite before Xenia woke up. So she put all her half-written letters in her suitcase, afraid to leave them in case he read her emotional ramblings, and then she put her coat on.

She left the letter for Dominic on her pillow and studied it in silence for a long moment. Then she went into the living-room, propped a letter of resignation, apology and regret on the mantelpiece, and hoped Xenia would understand.

Letting herself out of the suite, she went along the silent corridor to the silent lifts, and down to the foyer.

A handful of staff eyed her as she walked past with her suitcase, and she spoke briefly to the desk clerk, who ordered a taxi to take her to the airport.

When it arrived, she asked the driver to take her via St Isaac's Square, the Winter Palace, and the Nevsky Prospect, to give her one last glimpse of her beloved St Petersburg.

How beautiful it all was, particularly in the cool early-morning light, and she smiled at the gold spire of the Peter and Paul fortress, sparkling away across the river.

Greater tragedies than mine have happened here, she thought. Three thousand peasants dying in order that this city be built. Tsar Alexander II blown up and carried bleeding across the snow, to the Winter Palace, to die. Revolution pouring through the streets, leading to a new order and the death of the Tsar.

And last, but by no means least, her great-grandmother fleeing the smoke-filled city with a four-year-old daughter, a Fabergé music box, and memories of her beloved prince.

I may be suffering deeply from unrequited love, she thought, but I must be brave, I must try not to mind too much. At least I'm young, free and alive, even if I do love a man who will never, ever, ever love me.

Then the car headed out of town, and her heart ached with despair as she said goodbye inside herself to St Petersburg, to Dominic, and to her brief glimpse of happiness.

At the airport, she could do nothing but sit and wait.

It was a small building, an echoing beige-stone hall decorated with colourful wall friezes depicting aeroplanes during the war, and the people watching them fly overhead had a united zeal reminiscent of paintings of the French revolution.

Time ticked by.

She imagined Dominic going into her bedroom, finding the note. She felt sick inside at the thought of it. But why not tell him, in the end? After all, she would never see him again, so what difference would it make?

'... departure of British Airways flight...'

Natasha got to her feet, boarding pass, ticket, visa and exit form in one shaking hand. She began to walk towards Passport Control, her face white and cold.

'Natasha!' The dark, passionate voice stopped her in her tracks.

She froze with horror, whirling round to stare, seeing him run towards her across the Spartan hall, dressed in black, his coat flying apart as he ran, eyes blazing with blue fire.

'Don't!' she whispered as he reached her. 'Please, I can't bear it!'

'Natasha, you don't understand!' He gripped her shoulders, breathing hard. 'I read your note and——'

'But don't you see that's why I have to leave? If I stay I'll only get hurt, so badly hurt that I can't bear to face it, to let it happen, to be that——'

'I'm in love with you,' he said hoarsely.

Natasha fell silent, staring in disbelief into that tough, passionate face.

'I love you,' he said, and his voice shook low and ragged. 'I've loved you all along. I fell in love with you when I first saw you, standing in that lift, staring up at me with those strange eyes of yours, but I didn't realise it at the time, I didn't realise I loved you until that night I came to your flat, that first night——' He broke off, drawing a hoarse breath, his eyes fierce with emotion. 'Say something, for God's sake! Tell me I haven't just made a colossal fool of myself!'

'Darling!' she cried hoarsely, and flung her arms around his strong neck, kissing him so passionately she thought she'd die. 'I love you, I love you!' she kept saying against his mouth. 'Dominic, I love you, I love you, I love you...'

He groaned deeply, opening her mouth with his, crushing her against his body with love, not passion, his eyes as tightly closed as hers.

When she wrenched her bruised, dark mouth from his, she whispered, 'I can't believe this is happening. I can't believe it's real.'

He cradled her in his arms, kissing her head. 'Neither can I. I was so used to fighting you that I couldn't believe what I read in that note. I had to re-read it seven or eight times before I believed it. I nearly believed it was a lie. I nearly believed you'd written it just to save my feelings in the wake of your departure.'

'How could you believe that?' She stared at him hungrily. 'After last night, after I let you——'

'But don't you see, it was last night that crucified me? I couldn't resist making love to you, but I should never have done it without telling you how I felt first.'

'It crucified me too,' she whispered, tracing his face with one hand. 'I couldn't stop crying, all night. I didn't sleep at all.'

'Neither did I,' he said thickly, darkness haunting his eyes. 'The way you cried, the way you left, the way you agreed to be my mistress without love... I wanted to kill myself. I couldn't bear to face the fact that you were only physically attracted to me, that there might never be any love from you, never, not a shred of it——'

'But I only behaved like that because I was so afraid to tell you I loved you, and I had to get out of that bedroom before I broke down again.'

'You planned to leave then, didn't you?' He watched her with bruised eyes. 'Even while I was still inside you, you were planning to leave St Petersburg and me forever.'

'Yes... but I couldn't bear to stay another second. We'd made love so angrily, with so much hatred, and, however exciting it was at the time, the emptiness afterwards was crushing.'

'The expense of spirit in a waste of shame...' Dominic winced, bent his head, kissed her tenderly. 'My darling, please let me make it up to you. Let me make love to you properly, with real love, not hidden. I swear I'll never make you feel that way again.'

'Oh, darling...' She opened her mouth to his kiss, and they clung together in the draughty airport building, passionate lovers oblivious to everyone around them.

When Dominic raised his head, he was darkly flushed. 'Let's get back to the hotel at once. I have to be alone with you.'

He retrieved her case from the British Airways staff, and fifteen minutes later they were outside in the warm morning sunshine, the limousine parked opposite the airport steps by the trees and the green.

'When did you realise you loved me?' he asked, holding her hand with long fingers as the limousine drove slowly over to them.

'I knew it from the beginning,' she admitted huskily, smiling up at him with her obsessive green eyes.

'Did you?' He laughed softly with wonder, staring at her.

'I think so. Looking back, I did. I certainly wandered out of your office in a daze, dreaming mad dreams of love, and thinking you were the most gorgeous man I'd ever seen.'

'Oh, God!' He kissed her mouth burningly, moved by her declaration. 'I was just as hooked, just as enchanted...' he said against her mouth as his arms slid around her with passionate desire.

The chauffeur waited politely, and they broke apart, laughing. Her case was stowed in the boot, then they clambered into the rear of the limousine like children, laughing together, kissing each other, safe in the circle of each other's arms.

'So when did you admit it to yourself?' His eyes shone blue as the Neva river. 'I must know the exact moment!'

'It was last night.' Her fingers twined trustingly with his. 'I'd known it for ages already, but I was so afraid of saying it out loud in my own head because it seemed so impossible, so dangerous...'

'I've been afraid, too,' he said deeply. 'You weren't alone. Falling in love is something so unstoppable and uncontrollable that all you can do is pray you don't get smashed to pieces. Much like realising your car's going to crash and there's nothing you can do about it. Just hope you survive.'

'I was so convinced that all you wanted was sex.'

'Your fear worked in my favour,' he agreed softly, kissing her. 'It was easy at first for me to keep the pretence up, but the more you believed it, the harder it got.'

'I believed it implicitly.'

'I kept thinking I'd never have the courage or the opportunity to break through and tell you the truth. And in the end I was so badly hurt that I wanted to hurt you, because I thought it might make you break, tell me you loved me.'

She smiled up at him, helpless with love, and prepared to be so. 'It worked didn't it? That's exactly what I did in the end.'

'Yes.' He kissed her again, smiling. 'Thank God you did.'

'It was because I couldn't just leave you, not like that, not without saying something. You've done so much for me, darling. How could I just walk away from you? I had to let you know that I was leaving with love in my heart, not hate or anger or pride or fear. Just love.'

'You must have known,' he murmured, 'somewhere deep inside that I did love you.'

'Yes, I knew,' she said softly, eyes smiling. 'I don't know how and I don't even know that I really ever admitted it to myself. Certainly not when I wrote that note. But I must have known; you're right.'

'And I knew, deep inside, that you *did* love me. But it's a strange feeling, and so inexplicable. You sense it instinctively, even when there's nothing left to believe in, no evidence of love, not a shred of tangible proof. You just know.'

'Was there anything in particular that gave me away?' she asked huskily.

He studied her, his face deeply emotional. 'Your eyes... the way you used to look at me... such dark, obsessive hunger... How could any woman look at me that way and not love me?'

Natasha melted into his arms, raining kisses on his rough-hewn cheekbones, his strong jaw, his handsome mouth, and as he kissed her tenderly, she wrapped her arms around his neck.

The kiss took fire as the limousine swept serenely back to St Petersburg.

The Hotel Europe gleamed in the sunlight, and as they walked hand in hand across the marble foyer, it all seemed so different, so wonderful, the whole world refreshed and reborn in the light of true love.

They kissed in the lift as it rode up, and fell out of it together, oblivious to the chambermaid who smiled at the sight of them rushing to his suite along the corridor.

'Bedroom, darling,' he said deeply as they entered the suite. 'I need to be as alone with you as it's possible to be.'

They went inside and locked the door unnecessarily, bolting themselves up together in their intense, private world, kissing passionately as they took each other's clothes off, falling on to the bed, whispering their love, moving together as excitement took that intense, hair-raising grip which compelled nothing less than that they make love with open, honest, all-consuming passion.

It was real lovemaking, and so intensely personal that Natasha sobbed throughout orgasm with the sharpness of her release, gripping his shoulders and crying out his name in hoarse gasps of disbelief that this could be real.

When they collapsed, spent, in shuddering heat together, he kissed her deeply and said, 'I think I've been lonely all my life. I didn't realise it until I met you. Now that I've found you, please don't ever go away.'

'Darling,' she whispered, stroking his dark hair, 'I'll never leave you unless you stop loving me.'

'That'll never happen. My whole life makes sense if you love me. But if you don't love me, it's just a meaningless series of events.'

'I feel the same. In fact, I had a dream about——'

The telephone shrilled into the bedroom, making them both jump as it shattered their intimacy unwelcomely.

'Damn!' he said irritably, reaching for the receiver. 'Should have switched the bloody thing off!' He picked it up though and said coolly, '*Da*?'

Natasha traced the contours of his chest dreamily, then tensed as she heard his voice.

'Oh, hello, Kyra.' He made a face at Natasha, smiling wryly. 'No, I'm afraid I can't. Yes, I'm very busy. Well—for the rest of my life, really.'

Her eyes stared with dark jealousy and uncertainty at his face, praying she had not made a mistake.

'That's right...' Dominic was saying. 'Natasha. Well, I hope so. Yes, of course I'm serious! No, I haven't asked her yet, but I'm just about to.'

Her heart leapt with wild hope as she stared fixedly at him.

'No hard feelings at all, Kyra,' Dominic said. 'It's definitely not necessary. Oh, I understand better than you think. There's no need to explain. Yes, I'll see you around. Take care. *Dosvedenya...*'

Natasha watched him intently as he replaced the receiver. Her heart was beating fast. 'Well?' she asked, eyes fierce green with fear, jealousy, love.

'That was Kyra,' he said softly, moving back to kiss her. 'She wanted to see me while I'm here, to explain why she'd behaved the way she did years ago. The irony is that she sounded seductive. Obviously, she's changed her mind somewhere along the way, but I couldn't be less interested, and of course I said no.'

'And you said no because...' she whispered, holding her breath.

'Because I'm in love with you, Natasha. And I want to spend the rest of my life with you.'

'You—you said something to her about asking me something...?'

'Well, what do you think I might be about to ask you?' he murmured softly, smiling.

'I...' She moistened her lips, heart beating wildly.

'Shall I ask you here?' His blue eyes blazed with love. 'Or would you rather I proposed to you in Winter Palace Square?'

'Oh, Dominic!' She closed her eyes with intense love, her arms around him and her face buried in his neck, kissing him. 'Yes, I will marry you. A thousand times, over and over, for all eternity.'

'And when I die,' he asked shakingly, 'will you still love me?'

'I'll wait for you in the shadows of the afterlife,' she whispered. 'I'll come back to you in the next incarnation. I'll be yours forever, and I'll know you in three thousand years by the way you kiss me.'

'And I'll know you,' he said hoarsely, 'when I meet a girl with strange green eyes that stare at me with such dark, dark hunger...'

Natasha kissed him passionately, and as his body stirred hard with desire inside her, she thought of all the hell she had been through in her life, saw it suddenly as beautiful, wonderful, magical, because it had all been leading to this, and to the man who would ease her loneliness forever with his love.

His dark, obsessive love...

MILLS & BOON

CHRISTMAS CRACKERS

*A cracker of a gift pack full of
Mills & Boon goodies. You'll find...*

Passion—in *A Savage Betrayal* by Lynne Graham

A beautiful baby—in *A Baby for Christmas* by Anne McAllister

A Yuletide wedding—in *Yuletide Bride* by Mary Lyons

A Christmas reunion—in *Christmas Angel* by Shannon Waverly

Special Christmas price of 4 books for £5.99 (usual price £7.96)

Published: November 1995

*Available from WH Smith, John Menzies, Volume One, Forbuoys, Martins,
Tesco, Asda, Safeway and other paperback stockists.*

Christmas Journeys

4 new short romances all wrapped up in 1 sparkling volume.

Join four delightful couples as they journey home for the festive season—and discover the true meaning of Christmas...that love is the best gift of all!

A Man To Live For - Emma Richmond

Yule Tide - Catherine George

Mistletoe Kisses - Lynsey Stevens

Christmas Charade - Kay Gregory

Available: November 1995   **Price: £4.99**

MILLS & BOON

GET 4 BOOKS
AND A MYSTERY GIFT

Return this coupon and we'll send you 4 Mills & Boon Romances and a mystery gift absolutely FREE! We'll even pay the postage and packing for you.

We're making you this offer to introduce you to the benefits of Reader Service: FREE home delivery of brand-new Mills & Boon romances, at least a month before they are available in the shops, FREE gifts and a monthly Newsletter packed with information.

Accepting these FREE books and gift places you under no obligation to buy, you may cancel at any time, even after receiving just your free shipment. Simply complete the coupon below and send it to:

MILLS & BOON READER SERVICE, FREEPOST, CROYDON, SURREY, CR9 3WZ.

No stamp needed

Yes, please send me 4 free Mills & Boon Romances and a mystery gift. I understand that unless you hear from me, I will receive 6 superb new titles every month for just £1.99* each postage and packing free. I am under no obligation to purchase any books and I may cancel or suspend my subscription at any time, but the free books and gifts will be mine to keep in any case. (I am over 18 years of age)

2EP5R

Ms/Mrs/Miss/Mr _____

Address _____

_____

_____ Postcode _____

mps
MAILING
PREFERENCE
SERVICE

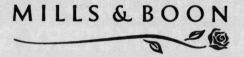

MILLS & BOON

Next Month's Romances

Each month you can choose from a wide variety of romance with Mills & Boon. Below are the new titles to look out for next month.

DARK FEVER	Charlotte Lamb
NEVER A STRANGER	Patricia Wilson
HOSTAGE OF PASSION	Diana Hamilton
A DEVIOUS DESIRE	Jacqueline Baird
STEAMY DECEMBER	Ann Charlton
EDGE OF DECEPTION	Daphne Clair
THE PRICE OF DECEIT	Cathy Williams
THREE TIMES A BRIDE	Catherine Spencer
THE UNLIKELY SANTA	Leigh Michaels
SILVER BELLS	Val Daniels
MISTRESS FOR HIRE	Angela Devine
THE SANTA SLEUTH	Heather Allison
AN IRRESISTIBLE FLIRTATION	Victoria Gordon
NEVER GO BACK	Anne Weale
THE MERMAID WIFE	Rebecca Winters
SOCIETY PAGE	Ruth Jean Dale